Christmas Miracles in Maternity

*Hope, magic and precious new beginnings
at Teddy's!*

Welcome to Teddy's Centre for Babies and
Birth, where the brightest stars of neonatal
and obstetric medicine work tirelessly to
save tiny lives and deliver bundles of joy all
year round—but there's never a time quite as
magical as Christmas!

Although the temperature might be
dropping outside, unexpected surprises
are heating up for these dedicated pros! And
as Christmas Day draws near secrets are
revealed, hope is ignited and love takes over.

Cuddle up this Christmas with the
heart-warming stories of the doctors, nurses,
midwives and surgeons at Teddy's in the
Christmas Miracles in Maternity miniseries:

The Nurse's Christmas Gift
by Tina Beckett

The Midwife's Pregnancy Miracle
by Kate Hardy

White Christmas for the Single Mum
by Susanne Hampton

A Royal Baby for Christmas
by Scarlet Wilson

All available now!

Dear Reader,

I always love writing Christmas stories—and what could be more fun than having a prince in your Christmas story?

This story is part of a series—Christmas Miracles in Maternity—set in the fictional Teddy's hospital in the Cotswolds. My heroine is feisty Scotswoman Sienna McDonald. She's always been focused completely on her career and is a dedicated neonatal cardiothoracic surgeon. Nothing gets between her and her babies!

Prince Sebastian meets Sienna unexpectedly and they spend two electrifying days together. He can't get her out of his head, even though he's expected to form an alliance by marrying a princess from another country. When he finds out Sienna is pregnant he's a man on a mission—to win the heart of the mother of his child!

I love to hear from readers. You can contact me via my website: scarlet-wilson.com.

Happy Christmas!

Scarlet

A ROYAL BABY
FOR CHRISTMAS

BY
SCARLET WILSON

First published in Great Britain 2016
By Mills & Boon, an imprint of HarperCollins*Publishers*
1 London Bridge Street, London, SE1 9GF

Large Print edition 2017

© 2016 Harlequin Books S.A.

Special thanks and acknowledgement are given to Scarlet Wilson for her contribution to the Christmas Miracles in Maternity series.

ISBN: 978-0-263-06702-6

Printed and bound in Great Britain
by CPI Antony Rowe, Chippenham, Wiltshire

Scarlet Wilson wrote her first story aged eight and has never stopped. She's worked in the health service for twenty years, trained as a nurse and a health visitor. Scarlet now works in public health and lives on the West Coast of Scotland with her fiancé and their two sons. Writing medical romances and contemporary romances is a dream come true for her.

Books by Scarlet Wilson

Mills & Boon Medical Romance

Midwives On-Call at Christmas
A Touch of Christmas Magic

Christmas with the Maverick Millionaire
The Doctor She Left Behind
The Doctor's Baby Secret
One Kiss in Tokyo…

Mills & Boon Cherish

Tycoons in a Million
Holiday with the Millionaire
A Baby to Save Their Marriage

Visit the Author Profile page at millsandboon.co.uk for more titles.

This book is dedicated to my fellow authors
Kate Hardy, Tina Beckett and
Susanne Hampton. It's been a pleasure
working with you, ladies!

**Praise for
Scarlet Wilson**

'The book is filled with high-strung emotions,
engaging dialogue, breathtaking descriptions
and characters you just cannot help but love.
With the magic of Christmas as a bonus, you
won't be disappointed with this story!'

—*Goodreads* on
A Touch of Christmas Magic

'*200 Harley Street: Girl from the Red Carpet*
is a fast-paced and feel-good medical
romance that sparkles with red-hot sensuality,
mesmerising emotion and intense passion.'

—*Goodreads*

'I am totally addicted to this author's books.
Not once have I picked up a book by her and
felt disappointed or let down. She creates
intense, perfect characters with so many
amazing levels of emotion it blows my mind
time and time again.'

—*Contemporary Romance Reviews* on
Tempted by Her Boss

PROLOGUE

May

HIS EYES SCANNED the bar as he ran his fingers through his hair. Six weeks, three countries, ten flights and thousands of miles. He'd been wined and dined by heads of state and consulate staff, negotiated trade agreements, arranged to be part of a water aid initiative, held babies, shaken hands for hours and had a number of tense diplomatic conversations.

All of this while avoiding dozens of calls from his mother about the upcoming royal announcement. His apparent betrothal to his lifelong friend.

All he wanted to do was find a seat, have a drink and clear a little head space. Il Palazzo di Cristallo was one of the few places he could do that. Set in the stunning mountains of Montanari, the exclusive boutique hotel only ever had a select few guests—most of whom were seeking sanctuary from the outside world. The press were banned. The staff were screened and well looked after to ensure all guests' privacy was well respected—including the Crown Prince of Montanari. For the first time in six weeks Sebastian might actually be able to relax.

Except someone was sitting in his favourite seat at the bar.

There. A figure with shoulders slumped and her head leaning on her hand. Her ash-blonde hair was escaping from its clasp and her blue dress was creased. Two empty glasses of wine sat on the bar in front of her.

The bartender sat down a third and gave Sebastian an almost indiscernible nod. The staff here knew he liked to keep his identity quiet.

Odd. He didn't recognise the figure. Sebastian knew all the movie stars and celebrities who usually stayed here. She wasn't a fellow royal or a visiting dignitary. His curiosity was piqued.

He strode across the room and slid onto the stool next to hers at the bar. She didn't even look up in acknowledgement.

Her fingers were running up and down the stem of the glass and her light brown eyes were unfocused. But it wasn't the drink. It was deep contemplation.

Sebastian sucked in a breath. Whoever she was, she was beautiful. Her skin was flawless. Her features finer than those of some of the movie starlets he'd been exposed to. Being Prince of Montanari meant that a whole host of women had managed to cross his path over the last few years. Not that he'd taken any of them seriously. He had a duty to his future kingdom. A duty to marry an acceptable neighbouring princess. There was no question about it—it had been instilled in him from a young age it was part of his preparations for finally becoming King. Marriage was a business transaction. It wasn't the huge love and undying happiness portrayed in fairy tales. There were no rainbows and flying unicorns. It came down to the most advantageous match for the country and his parents had found her. Theresa Mon Carte, his childhood friend and a princess from the neighbouring principality. They were to be married within the year.

Part of the reason he was here was to get some time to resign himself to his fate. Because that was what it felt like.

But right now, he couldn't think about that at all.

He was entirely distracted by the woman sitting next to him. She looked as if she had the weight of the world on her shoulders. There was no Botox here. Her brow was definitely furrowed and somehow he knew this woman would never be interested in cosmetic procedures.

'Want to tell me about them?'

'What?' She looked up, startled at the sound of his voice.

Light brown eyes that looked as if they'd once had a little dark eyeliner around them. It was smudged now. But that didn't stop the effect.

It was like being speared straight through the heart.

For a second neither of them spoke. It was the weirdest sensation—as if the air around them had just stilled.

He was drinking in everything about her. Her forgotten-about hair. Her crumpled clothes. Her dejected appearance.

But there was something else. Something that wouldn't let him break their gaze. A buzz. An air. He'd never felt something like this before. And she felt it too.

He could tell. Her pupils dilated just a little before his eyes. He didn't have any doubt that his were so big right now the Grand Canyon could fit in them.

There was something about her demeanour. This woman was a professional. She was educated. And she was, oh, so sexy.

He found his tongue. 'Your worries.' He couldn't help but let the corners of his mouth turn upwards.

She gave the briefest rise of her eyebrows and turned back towards the waiting wine glass. Her shoulders straightened a little. He'd definitely caught her attention.

Just as she'd caught his.

He leaned a little closer and nudged her shoulder. 'You're sitting on my favourite bar stool.'

'Didn't have your name on it,' she quipped back.

Her accent. It was unmistakeable. The Scottish twang made the hairs on his arms stand on end. He could listen to that all day. Or all night.

She swung her legs around towards him and leaned one arm on the bar. 'Come to think of it, you must be kind of brave.' She took a sip of her wine. Her eyebrows lifted again. 'Or kind of stupid.'

He liked it. She was flirting back. He leaned

his arm on the bar too, so they were closer than ever. 'What makes you think that?'

She licked her lips. 'Because you're trying to get between a Scots girl and the bar.' She smiled as she ran her eyes up and down the length of his body. It was almost as if she'd reached her fingers out and touched him. 'Haven't you heard about Scots girls?'

He smiled and leaned closer. 'I think I might need a little education.' He couldn't think of anything he wanted more.

Instant attraction. He'd never really experienced it before. Not like this. He'd wanted to come in here to hide and get away from things. Now, his sanctuary had become a whole lot more exciting.

A whole lot more distracting.

His stomach flipped over. What if he never felt like this again? Or even worse, what if he felt like this when he was King of Montanari and married?

Right now he was none of those things. The engagement hadn't been announced. He was about to step into a life of duty and constant scrutiny.

Theresa was a friend. Nothing more. Nothing less. They'd never even shared a kiss.

He hadn't come here to meet anyone. He hadn't come here to be attracted to someone.

But right now he was caught in a gaze he didn't want to escape from. The pull was just too strong.

Something flitted across her eyes. It was as if her confidence wavered for a second.

'What's wrong?' He couldn't help himself.

She sucked in a breath. 'Bad day at the office.'

'Anything to do with a man?' It was out before he thought.

She blinked and gave a little smile again, pausing for a second. 'No. Definitely nothing to do with a man.'

It was as if he'd just laid himself bare. Finding out the lie of the land. He couldn't ignore the warm feeling that spread straight through him.

He had no royal duties this weekend. There were no hands he needed to shake. No business he needed to attend to. He'd told Security he was coming here and to keep their distance.

If he lived to be a hundred he'd remember this. He'd remember this meeting and the way it made him feel. The buzz was so strong the air practically sparkled around her.

He was still single. He could do this. Right now

he would cross burning coals to see what would happen next.

He leaned even closer. 'I came here to get some peace and quiet. I came here to get some head space.' He gave her a little smile and lowered his voice. 'But, all of a sudden, there's no space in my head at all.'

He took a chance. 'How about I stop searching for some peace and quiet, and you forget all about your bad day?'

She ran her fingers up the stem of her wine glass. He could tell she was thinking. She looked up from beneath heavy eyelids. 'You mean, like a distraction. An interlude?'

The warm glow in his body started to rapidly rise. He nodded. 'A distraction.'

She licked her lips again and he almost groaned out loud. 'I think a distraction might be just what I need,' she said carefully.

He tried to quieten the cheerleader squad currently yelling in his head.

'I've always wanted to meet a Scots girl. Will you teach me how to wear a kilt?' He waved to the barman. 'There are some killer cocktails in here. You look like a Lavender Fizz kind of girl.'

'I'll do better than that.' There was a hint of mischief in her voice. 'I'll teach you how to take it off.'

This wasn't her life. It couldn't be. Things like this didn't happen to Sienna McDonald. But it seemed that in the blink of an eye her miserable, lousy day had just got a whole lot better.

It was the worst kind of day. The kind of day she should have got used to in this line of work.

But a doctor who got used to a baby dying was in the wrong profession.

It had been little Marco's third op. He'd been failing all the time, born into the world too early with undeveloped lungs and a malformed heart; she'd known the odds were stacked against him.

Some people thought it was wrong to operate on premature babies unless there was a guarantee of a good outcome. But Sienna had seen babies who had next to no chance come through an operation, fight like a seasoned soldier and go on to thrive. One of her greatest successes was coming up on his fourth birthday and she couldn't be prouder.

Today had been draining. Telling the parents had been soul-destroying. She didn't usually drown her sorrows in alcohol, but tonight, in a strange country with only herself for company, it was the only thing that would do. She'd already made short work of the accompanying chocolate she'd bought to go with the wine. The empty wrappers were littered around her.

She sensed him as soon as he sat down next to her. There was a gentle waft of masculine cologne. Her eyes were lowered. It was easy to see the muscled thigh through the probably designer trousers. If he was staying in this hotel— he was probably a millionaire. She was just lucky the royal family were footing her bill.

When he spoke, his lilting Mediterranean accent washed over her. Thank goodness she was sitting down. There was something about the accent of the men of Montanari. It crossed between the Italian, French and Spanish of its surrounding neighbours. It was unmistakeable. Unique. And something she'd never forget.

She glanced sideways and once more sucked in her cheeks.

Nope. The guy who looked as if he'd just walked off some film set was still there. Any second now she'd have to pinch herself. This might actually be real.

Dark hair, killer green eyes with a little sparkle and perfect white teeth. She might not have X-ray vision but his lean and athletic build was clear beneath the perfectly tailored suit. If she were back in Scotland she'd tell him he might as well have *sex on legs* tattooed on his forehead. Too bad she was in a posh kingdom where she had to be a whole lot more polite than that.

He hadn't responded to her cheeky comment. For a millisecond he looked a little stunned, and then his shoulders relaxed a little and he nodded slowly. He was getting comfortable. Did he think the game was over?

She was just settling in for the ride. She didn't do this. She didn't *ever* do this. Pick up a man in a bar? Her friends would think she'd gone crazy. But the palms of her hands were tingling. She wanted to touch him. She wanted to feel his skin against hers. She wanted to know exactly what those lips tasted like.

He was like every erotic dream she'd ever had just handed to her on a plate.

She leaned her head on one hand and turned to face him. 'Who says I'm a cocktail kind of girl?'

He blinked. Her accent did that to people. It took their ears a few seconds to adjust to the

Scottish twang. He was no different from every other man she'd ever met. The edges of his mouth turned upwards at the sound of her voice. People just seemed to love the Scottish accent—even if they couldn't understand a word she said.

'It's written all over you,' he shot back. He mirrored her stance, leaning his head on one hand and staring at her.

There was no mistaking the tingling of her skin. Part of her stomach turned over. There was a tiny wash of guilt.

Today wasn't meant to be a happy day. Today was a day to drown her sorrows and contemplate if she could have done anything different to save that little baby. But the truth was she'd already done that. Even if she went back in time she wouldn't do anything different. Clinically, her actions had been everything they should have been. Little Marco's body had just been too weak, too underdeveloped to fight any more.

The late evening sun was streaming in the windows behind him, bathing them both in a luminescence of peaches and purples. Distraction. That was what this was. And right now she could do with a distraction.

Something to help her forget. Something to help

her think about something other than work. She was due to go home in a few days. She'd taught the surgeons at Montanari Royal General everything she could.

She let her shoulders relax a little. The first two glasses of wine were starting to kick in.

'I don't know that I'm a Lavender Fizz kind of girl.'

'Well, let's see what kind of girl you are.' The words hung in the air between them, with a hundred alternative meanings circulating in her mind. This guy was good. He was very good.

She half wished she'd changed after work. Or at least pulled a brush through her hair and applied some fresh make-up. This guy was impeccable, which made her wish she were too. He picked up the cocktail menu, pretending to peruse it, while giving her sideways glances. 'No,' he said decidedly. 'Not gin.' He paused a second. 'Hmm, raspberries, maybe. Wait, no, here it is. A peach melba cocktail.'

She couldn't help but smile as she raised her eyebrows. 'And what's in that one?'

He signalled the barman. 'Let's find out.'

Her smile remained fixed on her face. His confidence was tantalising. She sipped at her wine as she waited for the barman to mix the drinks.

'What's your name?' he asked as they waited. He held out his hand towards her. 'I'm Seb.'

Seb. A suitable billionaire-type name. Most of the men in this hotel had a whole host of aristocratic names. Louis. Alexander. Hugo. Augustus.

She reached out to take his hand. 'Sienna.'

His hand enveloped hers. What should have been a firm handshake was something else entirely. It was gentle. Almost like a caress. But there was a purpose to it. He didn't let go. He kept holding, letting the warmth of his hand permeate through her chilled skin. His voice was husky. 'You've been holding on to that wine glass too long.' Before she could reply he continued. 'Sienna. It doesn't seem a particularly Scottish name.'

A furrow appeared on his brow. As if he were trying to connect something. After a second, he shook his head and concentrated on her again.

She tried not to fixate on the fact her hand was still in his. She liked it. She liked the way this man was one of the most direct flirts she'd ever met. He could have scrawled his intentions towards her with her lipstick on the mirrored gantry behind the bar and she wouldn't have batted an eyelid because this was definitely a two-way street.

'It's not.' She let her thumb brush over the back of his hand. 'It's Italian.' She lifted her eyebrows. 'I was conceived there. By accident—of course,' she added.

A look of confusion swept his face as the barman set down the drinks, but he didn't call her on her comment.

Sienna had a wave of disappointment as she had to pull her hand free of his and she turned to the peach concoction on the bar with a glimpse of red near the bottom. She lifted the tiny straws and gave it a little stir. 'What is this, exactly?'

Those green eyes fixed on hers again. 'Peach nectar, raspberry puree, fresh raspberries and champagne.'

She took a sip. Nectar was right. It hit the spot perfectly. Just like something else.

'Are you here on business or pleasure, Sienna?'

She thought for a second. She was proud to be a surgeon. Most men she'd ever met had seemed impressed by her career. But tonight she didn't want to talk about being a surgeon. Tonight she wanted to concentrate on something else entirely.

'Business. But it's almost concluded. I go home in a few days.'

He nodded carefully. 'Have you enjoyed visiting Montanari?'

She couldn't lie. Even today's events hadn't taken the shine off the beautiful country that she'd spent the last few weeks in. The rolling green hills, the spectacular volcanic mountain peak that overlooked the capital city and coastline next to the Mediterranean Sea made the kingdom one of the prettiest places she'd ever visited. She took another sip of her cocktail. 'I have. It's a beautiful country. I'm only sorry I haven't seen enough of it.'

'You haven't?'

She shook her head. 'Business is business. I've been busy.' She stirred her drink. 'What about you?'

He had an air about him. Something she hadn't encountered before. An aura. She assumed he must be quite enigmatic as a businessman. He could probably charm the birds from the trees. At least, she was assuming he was a businessman. He looked the part and every other man she'd met in this exclusive hotel had been here to do one business deal or another.

But for a charmer, there was something else. An underlying sincerity in the back of his eyes. Somehow she felt if the volcanic peak overlooking the capital erupted right now she would be safe with this guy. Her instincts had always been good and it had been a long time since she'd felt like that.

'I've been abroad on business. I'm just back.'

'You stay here? In this hotel?'

He laughed and shook his head. 'Oh, no. I live…close by. But I conduct much of my business in this hotel.' He gave another gracious nod towards the barman. 'They have the best facilities. The most professional staff. I'm comfortable here.'

It was a slightly odd thing to say. But she forgot about it in seconds as the barman came back to top up their glasses.

She took a deep breath and stared at her glass. 'Maybe I should slow down a little.'

His gaze was steady. 'The drink? Or something else?'

There it was. The hidden question between them. She ran her finger around the rim of the glass. 'I came here to forget,' she said quietly, exposing more of herself than she meant.

Her other hand was on the bar. His slid over the top, intertwining his fingers with hers. 'And so did I. Maybe there are other ways to forget.'

She licked her lips, almost scared to look up and meet his gaze again. It would be like answering the unspoken question. The one she was sure that she wanted to answer.

His thumb slid under her palm, tracing little circles. In most circumstances it would be calming. But here, and now, it was anything but calming; it was almost erotic.

'Sienna, you have a few days left. Have you seen the mountains yet? How about I show you some of the hidden pleasures that we keep secret from the tourists?'

It was the way he said it. His voice was low and husky, sending a host of tiny shivers of expectation up her spine.

She could almost hear the voices of her friends in her head. She was always the sensible one. Always cautious. If she told this tale a few months later and told them she'd made her excuses and walked away...

The cocktail glass was glistening in the warm sunset. The chandelier hanging above the bar sending a myriad of coloured prisms of light around the room.

The perfect setting. The perfect place. The perfect man.

A whole host of distraction.

Exactly what she'd been looking for.

She threw back her head and tried to remember if she was wearing matching underwear. Not that it mattered. But somehow she wanted all her memories about this to be perfect.

She met his green gaze. There should be rules about eyes like that. Eyes that pulled you in and held you there, while all the time giving a mischievous hint of exactly what he was thinking.

She stood up from her bar stool and moved closer. His hand dropped from the bar to her hip. She brushed her lips against his ear. 'How many of Montanari's pleasures are hidden?'

There it was. The intent.

It didn't matter that her perfect red dress was hanging in the cupboard upstairs. It didn't matter that her matching lipstick was at the bottom of her bag. It didn't matter that her most expensive perfume was in the bathroom in her room.

Mr Sex-on-Legs liked her just the way she was.

He closed his eyes for a second. This time his

voice was almost a growl, as if he were bathing in what she'd just said. 'I could listen to your accent all day.'

She put her hand on his shoulder. 'How about you listen to it all night instead?'

And the deed was done.

CHAPTER ONE

SHE STARED AT the stick again.

Yep. The second line was still there.

It wasn't a figment of her imagination. Just as the missing period wasn't a dream and the tender breasts weren't a sign of an ill-fitting bra.

A baby. She was going to have a baby.

She stared out of her house window.

Her mortgage. She'd just moved in here. Her mortgage was huge. As soon as she'd seen the house she'd loved it. It was totally too big for one person—how ironic was that?—but she'd figured she'd have the rest of her life to pay for it. It was five minutes from Teddy's and had the most amazing garden with a pink cherry blossom tree at the bottom of it, and a little paved area at the back for sitting.

It was just like the house she'd dreamed of as a child. The house where she and her husband and children would stay and live happily ever after.

She sighed and put her head in her hands.

She was pregnant. Pregnant to Seb, the liar.

It made her insides twist and curl. She'd never quite worked out when he'd realised who she was, while she'd spent the weekend in blissful ignorance.

A weekend all the while holed up in the most beautiful mountain chalet-style house.

The days had been joyful. She'd never felt an attraction like it—immediate, powerful and totally irresistible. Seb had made her feel like the only woman in the world and for two days she'd relished it.

It was too good. Too perfect. She should have known. Because nobody could ever be *that* perfect. Not really.

She'd been surprised by his security outside the hotel. But then, lots of businessmen had bodyguards nowadays. It wasn't quite so unusual as it could have been.

And she hadn't seen any of the sights of Montanari. Once they'd reached his gorgeous house hidden in the mountains, the only thing she'd seen was his naked body.

For two whole days.

She squeezed her eyes closed for a second. It hurt to remember how much she'd loved it.

How many other woman had been given the same treatment?

She shook her head and shuddered. Finding out who he really was had ruined her memories of those two wonderful days.

Of those two wonderful nights...

She pressed her hand on her non-existent bump. *Oh, wow.* She was pregnant by a prince.

Prince Sebastian Falco of Montanari.

Some women might like that. Some women might think that was amazing. Right now she was wondering exactly why her contraceptive pill had failed. She'd taken it faithfully every day. She hadn't been sick. She hadn't forgotten. This wasn't deliberate. This absolutely wasn't a ploy to get pregnant by a prince. But what if he thought it was?

Her mind jumped back to her house. How much maternity leave would she get? How much maternity pay would she get—would it cover her mortgage? She'd used her savings as the deposit for the house—that, and the little extra she'd had left to update the bathroom and kitchen, meant her rainy-day fund was virtually empty.

She stood up and started pacing. Who would look after her baby when she returned to work?

Would she be able to return to work? She had to. She was an independent woman. She loved her career. Having a baby didn't mean giving up the job she loved.

She rested her hand against the wall of her sitting room. Maybe someone at the hospital could give her a recommendation for a childminder? The crèche at the hospital wouldn't be able to cater for on-calls and late night emergency surgeries. She'd need someone ultra flexible. There was so much to think about. So much to organise.

She couldn't concentrate. Her mind kept jumping from one thing to the other. Oh, no—was this the pregnancy brain that women complained about?

She couldn't have that. She didn't have time for that. She was a neonatal cardiothoracic surgeon. She was responsible for tiny lives. She needed to be focused. She needed to have her mind on the job.

She walked through to the kitchen. The calendar was lying on the kitchen table. It was turned to April—showing when she'd had her last period. It had been left there when the realisation had hit her and she'd rushed to the pharmacy for a pregnancy test. She'd bought four.

She wouldn't need them. She flicked forward. Last date of period, twenty-third of April. Forty weeks from then? She turned the calendar over, counting the weeks on the back. January. Her baby was due on the twenty-eighth of January.

She pushed open her back door and walked outside. The previous owners had left a bench seat, carved from an original ancient tree that had been damaged in a lightning strike years ago. She sat down and took some deep breaths.

It was a beautiful day. The flowers in her garden had all started to emerge. Fragrant red, pink and orange freesias, blue cornflowers, purple delphinium and multi-coloured peonies blossomed in pretty colours all around her, their scents permeating the air.

She smiled. The deep breathing was beginning to calm her. A baby. She was going to have a baby.

She closed her eyes and pressed her lips together as a wave of determination washed over her. Baby McDonald might not have been planned. But Baby McDonald would certainly be wanted.

He or she would be loved. Be adored.

A familiar remembrance of disappointment and

anger made her catch her breath. For as long as she could remember her parents had made it clear to her that she'd been a 'mistake'. They hadn't put it quite in as few words but the implication was always there. Two people who had never really wanted to be together but had done 'what was right'.

Except it wasn't right. It wasn't right at all. Anger and resentment had simmered from them both. The expression on her father's face when he had left on her eighteenth birthday had told her everything she'd ever needed to know—as had the relief on her mother's.

She'd been a burden. An unplanned-for presence.

Whether this baby was planned for or not, it would always feel loved, always feel wanted. She might not know about childcare, she might not know about maternity leave, she might not know about her mortgage—but of that one thing, she was absolutely sure.

Her brain skydived somewhere else. Folic acid. She hadn't been taking it. She'd have to get some. Her feet moved automatically. She could grab her bag; the nearest pharmacy was only a five-minute drive. She could pick some up and start taking it immediately. As she crossed the garden her eyes squeezed shut for a second. Darn it. Folic acid was essential for normal development in a baby. She racked her brains. What had she been eating these last few weeks? Had there been any spinach? Any broccoli? She'd had some, but she just wasn't sure how much. She'd had oranges and grapefruit. Lentils, avocados and peas.

She winced. She'd just remembered her intake of raspberries and strawberries. They'd been doused in champagne in Montanari. Alcohol. Another no-no in pregnancy.

At least she hadn't touched a drop since her return.

Her footsteps slowed as she entered the house again. Seb. She'd need to tell him. She'd need to tell him she was expecting his baby.

A gust of cool air blew in behind her, sending every hair on her arms standing on end. How on earth would she tell him? They hadn't exactly left things on good terms.

She sagged down onto her purple sofa for a few minutes. How did you contact a prince?

Oliver. Oliver Darrington would know. He was Seb's friend, the obstetrician who had arranged for her to go to Montanari and train the other paediatric surgeons. But how on earth could she ask him without giving the game away? Would she sound like some desperate stalker?

Oh, Olly, by the way...can I just phone your friend the Prince, please? Can you give me his number?

She sighed and rested her head backwards on the sofa watching the yellow ticker tape of the news channel stream past.

Her eyes glazed over. Last time she'd seen Seb she'd screamed at him. Hardly the most ladylike response.

It didn't matter that his lie had been by omission. That might even seem a tiny bit excusable now. But then, six weeks ago, rationality had left the luxurious chalet she'd found herself in.

It had been a simple mistake. The car driver— or, let's face it, he was probably a lot more than that—had given a nod and said *Your Highness* to something Seb had asked him.

The poor guy had realised his mistake right away and made a prompt exit. But it was too late. She'd heard it.

At first she'd almost laughed out loud. She'd been so relaxed, so happy, that the truth hadn't even occurred to her. 'Your Highness?' She'd smiled as she'd picked up her bags to go back in the house.

But the look of horror on Seb's face had caused her foot to stop in mid-air.

And just like today, the hairs on her arms had stood on end. Seb. Sebastian. The name of the Prince of Montanari. The person who'd requested she train the surgeons in his hospital. The mystery man that she'd never met—because he was doing business overseas.

Just like Seb.

She might as well have been plunged into a cold pool of glacier ice.

'Tell me you're joking?'

For the first time since she'd met him, his coolness vanished. He started to babble. *Babble.* His eyes darting from side to side but never quite meeting her gaze.

She dropped her bags at her feet on the stony path. 'You're not, are you?' He kept talking but she stopped listening. Her brain trying to make sense of what was going on.

'You're Sebastian Falco? *You're* the Prince?' She walked right up under his nose.

It must have been the way she'd said it. As if

it were almost impossible. As if he were the un-likeliest candidate in the world.

He let out a sigh and those forest-green eyes finally met hers. His head gave the barest shake. 'Is that so ridiculous?'

The prickling hairs on her arms spread. Like an infectious disease. Reaching parts of her body that definitely shouldn't feel like that.

Although the rage was building inside her, all that came out was a whisper. 'It's ridiculous to me.'

He blinked. She could see herself reflected in his eyes. Hurt was written all over her face. She hated feeling like that. She hated being emotion-ally vulnerable.

Her mother and father had lived a lie for eigh-teen years. She'd always promised herself that would never be her life. That would never be her relationship.

She'd thrown caution to the wind and lost. Big style.

He'd made a fool of her. And she'd let him.

'How could you?' she snapped. 'How could you lie to me? What kind of woman do you think I am?'

As she heard the words out loud she almost

wanted to hide. She knew exactly what kind of woman she'd been these last two days. One that acted as though this was nothing. She'd experienced a true weekend of passion and abandon. She'd pushed aside all thoughts of consequences and lost herself totally in him.

Ultimate fail.

Now she was looking into the eyes of a man who'd misled her. Let her think that this was something it was not.

He pulled his gaze away from hers, having the good shame to look embarrassed, and ran his hand through his thick dark hair.

But even that annoyed her. She'd spent all weekend running her own fingers through the same hair and right now she knew she'd never do that again.

He reached up and touched her shoulder. 'Sienna, I'm sorry.'

She pulled back as if he'd stung her and his eyes widened.

'Don't touch me. Don't touch me again. Ever!' She spun around and walked back inside.

She ignored everything around her. Ignored the soft sofas they'd spent many an hour on. Ignored the thick wooden table that they'd eaten more than their dinner from. Ignored the tangled sheets in the white and gold bedroom that told their own story.

She grabbed the few things she'd brought with her—and the few other things she'd bought—and started throwing them into her bag.

Seb rushed in behind her. 'Sienna, slow down. Things weren't meant to happen like this. I'm sorry. I am. I came to the hotel to get away. I came to think about some things.' He ran his fingers through his hair again. 'And then, when I got there, there was just…' he held his hands up towards her '…you,' he said simply.

She spun back around.

'I didn't realise right away who you were. I'd asked Oliver if he could send a surgeon to help with training. I'm the patron of the hospital and they only come to me when there are big issues. The hospital board were unhappy about all our neonates having to be transferred to France for cardiac surgeries. It was time to train our own surgeons—buy our own equipment. But once I'd made the arrangement with Oliver I hadn't really paid attention to all the details. Our hospital director took care of all those because I knew I wouldn't be here. I didn't even recognise your name straight away.'

She felt numb. 'You knew? You knew exactly who I was?'

He sighed heavily and his tanned face paled. 'Not until yesterday when you mentioned you were a surgeon.'

She gulped. She knew exactly what he wasn't saying. Not until after they'd slept together.

'Why didn't you tell me? Why didn't you tell me you knew Oliver yesterday?'

He shook his head. 'Because we'd already taken things further than either of us probably intended. We were in our own little bubble here. And I won't lie. I liked it, Sienna. I liked the fact it was just you and me and the outside world seemed as far away as possible.' He took a deep breath. 'I didn't want to spoil it.' He started pacing around. 'Do you know what it's like to have the eyes of the world constantly on you? Do you know what it's like when every time you even say hello to a woman it's splashed across the press the next day that she could be the next Queen?' The frustration was clearly spilling over.

'You expect me to feel sorry for you?'

He threw up his hands. 'The only time I've

had a bit of a normal life was when I was at university. The press were banned from coming near me then. But every moment before that, and every second after it, I've constantly been on display. Life is never normal around me, Sienna. But here—' he indicated the room '—and in Il Palazzo di Cristallo I get a tiny bit of privacy. Do you know how good it felt to walk in somewhere, see a beautiful woman and be able to act on it? Be able to actually let myself feel something?'

Her throat was dry. Emotion and frustration was written all over his face. He couldn't stop pacing.

It was as if the weight of the world were currently sitting on his shoulders. She had no idea what his life was like. She'd no idea what was expected of him. Her insides squirmed. The thought of constantly being watched by the press? No, thanks.

But the anger still burned inside. The hurt at being deceived. How many other women had he brought here? Was she just another on his list?

She stepped up close to him again, ignoring his delicious aftershave that had wound its way around her over the last few days. 'So, everything was actually a lie?'

He winced. 'It wasn't a lie, Sienna.'

'It was to me.'

He shook his head and straightened his shoulders. 'You're overreacting. Even if I had introduced myself, what difference would it have made?' He moved closer, his chest just in front of her face. 'Are you telling me that this wouldn't have happened? That we wouldn't have been attracted to each other? We wouldn't have ended up together?'

She clouded out his words—focusing only on the first part. It had been enough to make the red mist descend. 'I'm overreacting?' She dropped the clothes she had clutched in her hands. 'I'm overreacting?' She let out an angry breath as her eyes swept the room.

She shook her head. 'Oh, no, Seb. I'm not overreacting.' She picked up the nearest lamp and flung it at the wall, shattering it into a million pieces. '*This*. This is overreacting. This is letting you know how I really feel about your deception.'

His chin practically hung open.

She stalked back to the bed and stuffed the remaining few items into her bag, zipping it with an over-zealous tug.

She marched right up under his nose. 'If I never

see you again it will be too soon. Next time find someone else to train your surgeons. Preferably someone who doesn't mind being deceived and lied to.'

He drew himself up to his full height. On any other occasion she might have been impressed. But that day? Not a chance.

His mouth tightened. 'Have it your own way.'

'I will,' she'd shouted as she'd swept out of the chalet and back into the waiting car. 'Take me back to my hotel,' she'd growled at the driver.

Heavens. She hoped she hadn't got that poor man fired. He hadn't even blinked when she'd spoken. Just put the car into gear and set off down the mountain road. Her last view of Seb had been as he'd walked to the door and watched the car take off.

Now, it seemed all a bit melodramatic.

She'd never admit she'd cried on the plane on the way home. Not to a single person. And especially not to a person she'd now have to tell she was carrying his baby.

Her eyes came into focus sharply and she leaned forward.

The tickertape stream of news changed constantly. Something had made her focus again.

She waited a few seconds.

Prince Sebastian Falco of Montanari has announced his engagement to his childhood friend Princess Theresa Mon Carte of Peruglea. Although the date of their wedding has not yet been announced it is expected to be in the next calendar year. The royal wedding will unite the two neighbouring kingdoms of Montanari and Peruglea.

Every single tiny bit of breath left her body. Her stomach plummeted as a tidal wave of emotions consumed her.

It was as if the glacier ice pool she'd imagined on the mountain of Montanari had followed her home. Nausea made her bolt to the bathroom.

This wasn't morning sickness.

This was pure and utter shock.

He was engaged. Sebastian was engaged.

As she knelt on the bathroom floor she felt momentarily light-headed. Could this be any worse?

She squeezed her eyes closed. Trying to banish all the memories of that weekend from her mind. Her body responded automatically, curling into a ball on the ground. If she didn't think about him, she couldn't hurt. She couldn't let herself hurt like this. She had a baby. A baby to think about.

She pressed her head against the cool tiles on the wall.

Pregnant by a prince. An *engaged* prince.

Funnily enough, no fairy tale she'd ever heard of ended like this.

CHAPTER TWO

December

SHE WAS LATE. Again. And Sienna was never late. She hated people being late. And now she was turning into that person herself.

It was easy to shift the blame. Her obstetrician's clinic was running nearly an hour behind. How ironic. Even being friends with the Assistant Head of Obstetrics around here didn't give her perks—but she could hardly blame him. Oliver had been dealing with a particularly difficult case. It just meant that now she wouldn't complete her rounds and finish when planned.

She hurried across the main entrance of the hospital and tried not to be distracted by the surroundings. The Royal Cheltenham hospital—or Teddy's, as they all affectionately called it—did Christmas with style.

A huge tree adorned the glass atrium. Red and gold lights twinkled merrily against the already darkening sky. The tea room near the front entrance—staffed by volunteers—had its own display. A complete Santa sleigh and carved wooden reindeers with red Christmas baubles on their noses. Piped music surrounded her. Not loud enough to be intrusive, but just enough to set the scene for Christmas, as an array of traditional carols and favourite pop tunes permeated the air around her.

Sienna couldn't help but smile. Christmas was her absolute favourite time of year. The one time of year her parents actually stopped fighting. Her mother's sister, Aunt Margaret, had always visited at this time of year. Her warmth and love of Christmas had been infectious. As soon as she walked in the house, the frosty atmosphere just seemed to vanish. If Margaret sensed anything, she never acknowledged it. It seemed it wasn't the 'done thing' to fight and argue in front of Aunt Margaret and Sienna loved the fact that for four whole days she didn't have to worry at all.

Aunt Margaret's love of Christmas had continued—for Sienna, at least—long after she'd died. Sienna's own Christmas tree had gone up on the first of December. Multicoloured lights were decorating the now bare cherry blossom at the bottom of her garden. She wasn't even going to admit how they got there.

It seemed that Mother Nature was even trying to get in on the act. A light dusting of snow currently covered the glass atrium at Teddy's.

This time next year would be even more special. This time next year would be her baby's first Christmas. A smile spread across Sienna's face.

Thoughts like that made her forget about her aching back and sore feet. At thirty-four weeks pregnant she was due to start maternity leave some time soon. Oliver had arranged for some maternity cover, and he'd had the good sense to start her replacement early. Max Ainsley was proving more than capable.

He'd picked up the electronic systems and referral pathways of Teddy's easily. It meant that she'd be able to relax at home when the baby arrived instead of fretting over cancelled surgeries and babies and families having to travel for miles to get the same standard of care.

She hurried into the neonatal unit and stuffed her bag into the duty room. She looked up and took a deep breath. Every cot was full. An influx of winter virus had hit the unit a few weeks ago. That, along with delivery of a set of premature quads—one of whom needed surgery—meant that the staff were run off their feet.

Ruth, one of the neonatal nurses, shot her a sympathetic look. 'You doing okay, Sienna?'

Sienna straightened up and rubbed her back, then her protruding stomach. She was used to the sideways glances from members of staff. As she'd never dated anyone from the hospital and most of the staff knew she lived alone, speculation about her pregnancy had been rife.

The best rumour that she'd heard was that she'd decided she didn't need a man and had just used a sperm donor to have a baby on her own. If only it were true.

She'd stopped watching the news channel. Apart from weather reports and occasional badly behaved sportsmen, it seemed that her favourite news channel had developed an obsession with the upcoming royal wedding in Montanari early next year.

News was obviously slow. But if she saw one more shot of Seb with his arm around the cut-out perfect blonde she would scream. She didn't care that they looked a little awkward together. She just didn't want to see them at all.

She smiled at Ruth. 'I'm doing fine, thanks.

Just had my check-up. Six weeks to go.' She waved her hand at the array of cots. 'I've got three babies to review. I'm hoping we can get at least two of them home for their first Christmas in the next few days. What do you think?'

As she said the words her Head Neonatal Nurse appeared behind Ruth. She'd worked with Annabelle Ainsley for the last year and had been more than a little surprised when it had been revealed that Annabelle was actually Max's estranged wife. She hadn't been surprised that it had only taken them a week to reconcile once he'd started working at Teddy's. For the last couple of weeks Annabelle hadn't stopped smiling, so she was surprised to see her looking so serious this afternoon.

'There's someone here to see you.' The normally unfazed Annabelle looked a little uncomfortable.

Sienna picked up the nearest tablet to check over one of her patients. 'Who is it? A rep? Tell them I don't have time, I'm sorry.' She gave Annabelle a smile. 'I think I should maybe hand all the reps over to Max now—what do you think?'

Annabelle glanced at Ruth. 'It's not a rep. I don't recognise him and didn't have time to ask his name. He's insisting that he'll only speak to you and…' she took a breath '…he won't be kept waiting.'

Sienna sat the tablet back down, satisfied with the recordings. Her post-surgery baby was doing well. She shook her head. 'Well, who does he think he is?' She looked around the unit and paused. 'Wait? Is it a parent of one of the babies? Or someone with a surgery scheduled for their child? You know that I'll speak to them.'

Annabelle shook her head firmly. 'No. None of those. No parents—or impending parents. It's something else entirely.' She handed a set of notes to Ruth. 'Can you check on little Maisy Allerton? She didn't take much at her last feed.'

Ruth nodded and disappeared. Annabelle pressed her lips together. 'This guy, he says it's personal.'

Sienna felt an uncomfortable prickle across her skin. 'Personal? Who would have something personal to talk to me about?'

The words were out before she even thought about them. Nothing like making herself sound sad and lonely. Did people at Teddy's even think she had a personal life?

Annabelle's eyes darted automatically to Sienna's protruding stomach, then she flushed as she realised Sienna had noticed.

Sienna straightened her shoulders. She'd never been a fan of anyone trying to push her around. She gave Annabelle a wide smile. 'Oh, he's insisting, is he?'

Annabelle nodded then her eyes narrowed and she folded her arms across her chest. She'd worked with Sienna long enough to sense trouble ahead.

Sienna kept smiling. 'Well, in that case, I'll review my three babies. Talk to all sets of parents. I might make a few phone calls to some parents with babies on my list between Christmas and New Year, and then...' she paused as she picked up the tablet again to start accessing a file '...then, as a heavily pregnant woman, I think I'll go and have something to eat. I missed lunch and—' she raised her eyebrows at Annabelle '—I have a feeling a colleague I work with might *insist* I don't faint at work.'

Annabelle smiled too and nodded knowingly. 'Not that I want to be any influence on you, but the kitchen staff made killer carrot cake today. I think it could count as one of your five a day.'

Sienna threw back her head and laughed.

'You're such a bad influence but I could definitely be persuaded.' Her eyes went straight back to the chart. 'Okay, so let's see Kendall first. Mr I-Insist is just going to have to find out how things work around here.'

Annabelle gave a smile and put an arm at Sienna's back. 'Don't worry. Somehow I think you'll be more than a match for him. Give me a signal when you come back. I can always page you after five minutes to give you an escape.'

Sienna nodded. She didn't really care who was waiting for her—her babies would always come first.

Seb was furious. He kept glancing at his watch. He'd been in this room for over an hour—his security detail waiting outside.

The sister of the neonatal ward had seemed surprised at first by his insistence at seeing Sienna. Then, she'd explained Sienna was at another appointment and would be back soon. What exactly meant *soon* at the Royal Cheltenham?

He'd paced the corridors a few times looking for her with no success. The doors to the neonatal unit had a coded lock, and, from the look of the anxious parents hurrying in and out, it really wasn't a place he wanted to be.

He'd been stunned when Oliver Darrington had phoned him to discuss his own difficult situation—after a one-night stand a colleague was pregnant. A colleague who he had feelings for. Oliver had been Sebastian's friend since they'd attended university together, even though they were destined for completely different lives.

He hadn't told Oliver a thing about his weekend with Sienna, so when Oliver had mentioned that Sienna too was pregnant, Sebastian had felt as if he couldn't breathe.

His tongue had stuck to the roof of his mouth and his brain had scrambled to ask the question he'd wanted to, without giving himself away. According to Oliver she was heavily pregnant—due to have her baby at the end of January.

For a few seconds Seb had felt panicked. The dates fitted perfectly. He didn't have a single doubt that her baby could be his.

He could hardly remember the rest of the conversation with Oliver. That made him cringe now. It was a complete disservice to his friend.

He'd had things to deal with.

Since Sienna had stormed out of his chalet

retreat his life had turned upside down. He'd followed his parents' wishes and allowed the announcement of the engagement. Theresa had seemed indifferent. Uniting the kingdoms had been important to her too. But marrying someone she wasn't in love with didn't seem any more appealing to her than it was to him.

If Sienna hadn't happened, maybe, just maybe, he could have mustered some enthusiasm and tried to persuade Theresa their relationship could work.

But his nights had been haunted with dreams of being tangled in the sheets with a passionate woman with ash-blonde hair, caramel-coloured eyes and a firm, toned body.

She'd ignited a flame inside him. Something that had burned underneath the surface since she'd left. He'd been a fool. A fool to let his country think he would take part in a union he didn't think he could make work.

His parents had been beside themselves with anger at the broken engagement.

Theresa had been remarkably stoic about him breaking the engagement. She'd handed back the yellow diamond ring with a nod of her head. He suspected her heart lay somewhere else. Her voice had been tight. 'I hadn't got around to finalising the design for my wedding dress yet. The designer was furious with me. It's just as well really, isn't it?'

He'd felt bad as he bent to kiss her cheek. Theresa wasn't really upset with him. Not yet, anyway. She might be angrier when she found out about the baby. It could be embarrassing for her. He only hoped she would have moved on to wherever her heart truly lay.

The Head of his PR had nearly had a heart attack. He'd actually put his hand to his chest and turned an alarming shade of grey. And that had given Sebastian instant inspiration. In amongst breaking the news to both Theresa and his parents, Sebastian had spent the last two weeks doing something else—making arrangements to twin the Cheltenham hospital with the Montanari Royal General. He was already a patron of his own hospital; a sizeable donation would make him a patron of Teddy's too.

It was the perfect cover story. He could come to the Royal Cheltenham without people asking too many questions. Oliver had been surprised for around five minutes. Then, he'd made him an appointment with the board. In the meantime, Sebastian could come freely to the hospital with his security and press team in tow. The announcement was due to be made tomorrow. Seb was hoping he could also make an announcement of his own.

He glanced at his watch again as the anger built in his chest. Sienna hadn't even contacted him. Hadn't even let him know he was going to be a father. Was her intention to leave his child fatherless? For the heir of Montanari not to be acknowledged or have their rightful inheritance?

That could never happen. He wouldn't *allow* that to happen. Not in his lifetime.

He heard a familiar voice drifting down the corridor towards him. It sent every sense on fire. That familiar Scottish twang. The voice she'd invited him to listen to all night…

'No problem. I'll be along to review the chest X-ray in five minutes. Thanks, Max.'

The footsteps neared but he wasn't prepared for the sight. Last time he'd seen Sienna she'd been toned and athletic. This time the rounded belly appeared before she did.

Her footsteps stopped dead in the doorway, her eyes wide. It was clear he was the last person she'd been expecting to see.

She took his breath away. She didn't have on a traditional white coat. Instead she was dressed in what must be a maternity alternative to a suit. Black trousers with a matching black tunic over the top. It was still smart. Still professional. Her hair was gleaming, a bit longer than he remembered and tucked behind her ears. A red stethoscope hung around her neck, matching her bright red lipstick.

'Sebastian.' It was more a breath than a word.

Her hand went automatically to her stomach. His reply stuck in his throat. He hadn't been ready. He hadn't been ready for the sight of her ripe with his child. Even under her smart clothes he could see her lean body had changed totally. Her breasts were much bigger than before—and they suited her. Pregnancy suited her in a way he couldn't even have imagined.

But now he was here, he just didn't even know where to start.

This wasn't happening. Not here. Not now.

She'd planned things so carefully. All her surgeries were over. Any new patients had been seen jointly with Max. He would perform the neonatal surgeries and she would do later follow up once she was back from maternity leave.

But here he was. Right in front of her. The guy she'd spent the last six months half cursing, half pining for.

Those forest-green eyes practically swept up and down her body. Her palm itched. That thick dark hair. The hair she'd spent two days and two nights running her fingers through. Those broad shoulders, filling out the exquisitely cut suit. The pale lilac of the shirt and the shocking pink of his tie with his dark suit and good looks made him look like one of the models adorning the billboards above Times Square in New York. Imagine waking up with that staring in your hotel window every morning.

Her breath had left her lungs. It was unnatural. It was ridiculous. He was just a man. She sucked in a breath and narrowed her gaze. 'Congratulations on your engagement.'

He flinched. What had he expected? That she'd welcome him here with open arms?

Part of her felt a tiny twinge of regret. Her hand had picked up the phone more times than she could count. She'd tried to have that conversation with Oliver on a number of occasions. But it was clear that he'd never realised what was behind her tiny querying questions. The thought that his friend might have had a liaison with his colleague obviously hadn't even entered his mind.

Was it really such a stretch of the imagination? Sebastian let out a sigh and stepped towards her. She held up her hand automatically to stop him getting too close—last thing she needed was to get a whiff of that familiar aftershave. She didn't need any more memories of the past than she already had. Baby was more than enough.

The royal persona she'd seen on the TV news seemed to be the man in the room with her now. This wasn't the cheeky, flirtatious, incredibly sexy guy that she'd spent two days and two nights with. Maybe her Seb didn't really exist at all?

There was something else. An air about him she hadn't noticed before. Or maybe she hadn't been paying attention. An assurance. A confidence. The kind of persona that actually fitted with being a prince.

He caught the hand she held in front of her.

The effect was instant, a rush of warmth and a pure overload of memories of the last time he'd touched her.

If she hadn't been standing so squarely she

might have swayed. Her senses were alight. Now, his aftershave was reaching across the short space between them like a cowboy's rope pulling her in. Her hand tingled from where he held it. His grip initially had been firm but now it changed and his thumb moved under her palm, tracing circles—just as he'd done months ago.

Her breathing stalled. No. No, she wasn't going to go here again.

This was the man that had announced his engagement a few weeks after they'd met. An engagement to a childhood friend. Had he been seeing her the whole time? She'd checked. But the media wasn't sure. Had he been sleeping with them both at the same time?

She had no idea.

But no matter what her senses were doing, thoughts like that coloured her opinion of the man. He hadn't been honest with her. They hadn't promised each other anything, but that didn't matter.

She snatched her hand back.

'I'm not engaged, Sienna. I broke off my engagement when I heard the news you were pregnant.' His voice was as smooth as silk.

She felt herself bristle. 'And what am I supposed to feel—grateful?'

He didn't even blink. He just kept talking. 'I heard the news from Oliver. He called me about something else. A woman. Ella? Do you know her?'

Sienna frowned. 'Yes, yes, I know her. She's a midwife here.' She paused. Did Sebastian know the full story?

'They're engaged,' she said carefully, missing out the part that Ella was pregnant too. She wasn't sure just how much Oliver would have told Sebastian.

A wide smile broke across Sebastian's face. 'Perfect. I'll need to congratulate him.' His focus came back on Sienna. 'Maybe we could have a joint wedding?'

'A what?' Someone walking past the door turned their head at the rise of her voice. 'Are you crazy?'

Sebastian shook his head. 'Why would you think I'm crazy?'

He drew himself up in front of her. 'You're carrying the heir to the Montanari throne. We might still have things to sort out, but I'd prefer it if the heir to the throne was legitimate. Wouldn't you?

If you come back with me now we can be married as soon as we get there. We can tell the world we met when you came to work in Montanari Royal General. Everything fits.'

He made it all sound so normal. So rational. So matter-of-fact.

She wasn't hearing this. She wasn't. It was some sick, delusional dream. She thought back to everything she'd eaten today. Maybe she'd been exposed to something weird.

He reached into his pocket and pulled out a ring. 'Here.'

She wasn't thinking straight and held out her hand. 'What is it?'

One of the ward clerks walked past and raised her eyebrows at the sight of the way-too-big diamond. Perfect. Just perfect. She was already the talk of the place and Polly was the world's biggest gossip. She just prayed that Polly hadn't recognised Sebastian.

She flinched and pulled her hand away. 'What am I supposed to do with that?'

'Put it on,' he said simply, glancing at her as if it were a stupid question. 'You need to wear an engagement ring.' He paused for a second and looked at her face. 'Don't you like it? It's a family heirloom.' His forehead wrinkled. 'I'm sure I can find you something else in the family vault.'

She shook her head and started pacing. 'It doesn't matter if I like it. I don't want it. I don't need it. I'm—' She stopped and placed her hand on her stomach. *'We're* going nowhere. I have a job here. A home. The very last place I'm going is Montanari. And the very last thing I'm doing...' she paused again and shook her head, trying to make sense of the craziness around her. She drew in a deep breath and stepped right up to him, poking her finger in her chest. 'The very last thing I'm doing is marrying you.'

Now Sebastian started shaking his head. He had the absolute gall to look surprised. 'Why on earth not? You're expecting our child. You're going to be the mother of the heir to Montanari. We should get married. And as soon as possible.' He said it as if it made perfect sense.

Sienna put her hands on her back and started pacing. 'No. No, we absolutely shouldn't.'

Sebastian held out his hands. 'Sienna, in a few years you get to be the Queen of Montanari. What woman wouldn't want that?'

She shuddered. She actually shuddered. 'Oh, no. Oh, no.'

Sebastian's brow creased. 'What on earth is wrong? We can have a state wedding in Montanari...' he glanced at her stomach and gave a little shrug '...but we'll need to be quick.'

Sienna took a step back. 'Okay, were you really this crazy when I met you in Montanari and I just didn't notice? Because this is nowhere near normal.' She put her hand on her stomach. 'Yes, I'm pregnant. Yes, I'm pregnant with your baby. But that's it, Sebastian. This isn't the Dark Ages. I don't want your help—or need it.' She ran her fingers through her hair, trying to contemplate all the things she hadn't even considered. 'Look at me, Sebastian. I live here. In the Cotswolds. I came here from Edinburgh. I purposely chose to come here. I've bought my dream house. I have a great job and colleagues that I like and admire. I've arranged a childcare for my baby and cover for my maternity leave.' She could feel herself getting agitated. Her voice was getting louder the longer that she spoke. 'I won't keep you from our baby. You can have as much—or as little— contact as you want. But don't expect to waltz in here and take over our lives.' She pressed her hand to her chest. 'This is my life, Sebastian. *My life.* I don't need your money and I don't need your help. I'm perfectly capable of raising this baby on my own.'

Polly walked past again. It was obviously deliberate. Not only was she spying, now she was eavesdropping too.

With a burst of pure frustration Sienna kicked the door closed.

Sebastian raised his eyebrows.

She took a deep breath. 'I need you to go. I need you to leave. I can't deal with this now.'

Her lips pressed tight together and resisted the temptation to say the words she was truly thinking.

Sebastian seemed to have frozen on the spot. The air of assurance had disappeared.

It was then she saw it. The look. The expression.

He'd actually expected her to say yes.

He hadn't expected her to reject him. He hadn't expected a no.

Sebastian Falco was hurt.

Now, it was her that was surprised. It struck her in a way she didn't expect. She could almost see a million things circulating around in his brain—as if he was trying to find a new way to persuade her to go with him.

She could see the little vein pulsing at the base of his throat.

Her mouth was dry.

If she were five years old—this would be her dream. Well, not the pregnancy, but the thought of a prince sweeping in and saying he would marry her, presenting her with a huge diamond ring and the chance to one day be Queen.

But it had been a long time since Sienna had been five.

And her ambitions and dreams had changed so much they could move mountains.

Sebastian folded his arms across his chest. 'Why didn't you call me, Sienna?' His voice was rigid. 'Why didn't you phone and tell me as soon as you knew you were pregnant?'

Oh. That.

She should have expected it to come up.

'I was going to. I meant to. But the day I did my pregnancy test was the day your engagement was announced on the national news.' She looked at him directly, trying to push away the tiny part of guilt curling in her stomach. 'Between that, and finding out I was pregnant, it kind of took the feet out from under me.'

He broke their gaze for a second, his words

measured. 'Theresa was a friend. It wasn't going to be a marriage of love. It was going to be a union of kingdoms. Something my parents wanted very much.'

'How romantic.'

She couldn't help herself. She'd been a child of a loveless marriage. She knew the effects it had. She raised her eyes to the ceiling. 'Well, your parents must be delighted about me. I guess I'm going to be the national scandal.'

She'd been delusional. She'd thought she knew this man—even a little. But nothing about this fitted with the two days they'd spent together. The Sebastian she'd known then was a man who actually felt and thought. He'd laughed and joked and made her the coffee she craved. He'd cuddled up beside her in bed and taken her to places she'd never been before. He'd gently stroked the back of her neck as she'd fallen asleep. He was someone she'd loved being around.

Too bad all of it had been a lie.

The man in front of her now was the Sebastian that appeared on the news. The one with a fixed smile and his arm around someone else.

That was what it was. That was what she'd always noticed. Even though she'd tried not to watch him on the news—she'd tried to always switch channel—on the few occasions she had seen pictures of him, something had never seemed quite right.

She'd always tried not to look too closely. Her heart wouldn't let her go there. Not at all.

But little things were falling into place.

The smile had never reached his eyes.

Now, the look in his eyes seemed sincere. His tone much softer. 'You can be whatever you want to be, Sienna. I'd just like you to do it as my wife.'

This look was familiar. She'd seen it so many times on the weekend they'd spent together. In between the flirting, fun and cheekiness there had been flashes of sincerity.

That had been the thing that made his untruthfulness so hard to take.

The room was starting to feel oh-so-small.

'Why didn't you call me later?'

It didn't matter that she'd just sipped some water. Her mouth felt dry. He wasn't going to let this go. He was calling her on it.

She licked her lips. 'I wanted to. I thought about it. But we didn't exactly exchange numbers. How easy is it to call a royal palace and ask to speak to the Prince?'

He shifted a little uncomfortably, then shook his head. 'You could have asked Oliver. You knew we were friends. He was the one who recommended you. He would have given you the number whenever you asked.'

'And how would that work out? "Oh, Oliver? Can you give me Seb's mobile number, please? I want to tell him that I'm going to ruin his engagement by letting him know I'm pregnant. You know, the engagement to his childhood sweetheart?" At least that's the way it sounded in the media.'

He smiled. He actually smiled.

'You think it's funny?'

'No. Not at all. But that's the first time you've called me Seb since I got here.' He stepped forward.

She sucked in a breath.

She hadn't even noticed.

Seb was too close again. She needed some space, some distance between them.

He touched her arm. Her bare skin almost caught fire. There was no opportunity to flinch or pull away. His palm surrounded her slim wrist. 'I've told you. It was never like that with Theresa. We just didn't think of each other that way.

And we'd never been childhood sweethearts. We were friends. Just friends.'

'You've told her about the pregnancy?'

He gave a little grimace. 'Not exactly. Not yet anyway.' He ran his fingers through his hair. 'I wasn't quite sure how to put it.'

'You were sleeping with us both?'

She couldn't help it. It just came out.

'What? No.' Sebastian shook his head again. 'I've never slept with Theresa. I've told you. It wasn't that kind of relationship. I don't sleep with my friends.'

She hated the way that relief flooded through her. The sincerity was written all over his face. He might have lied by omission before but she was certain he wasn't lying now.

She met his gaze. 'How will she feel when she finds out? It will look to the world as if you've made a fool of her. As if *we've* made a fool of her. I hate that. I don't want anyone to think I'd have an affair with someone else's man.'

He sucked in a deep breath and reached up towards her face. 'But I wasn't in a relationship with Theresa. I was single. I was free when we were together. And if I'd known you were pregnant I would never have let my parents force me into announcing an engagement.' His hand brushed her cheek and his fingers tangled in her hair.

This was what he'd done when they'd been together. This was how he'd pulled her into *that* first kiss.

The touch should have been mesmerising. But his words left her cold.

Forced. He'd never really mentioned his parents in their short time together.

'They forced you? I didn't think you'd let anyone force you to do anything.' There was an air of challenge in her voice.

He recognised it and raised his eyebrows. He gave her a half-smile. 'You haven't met my parents—yet.'

It was her first truly uncomfortable feeling. The King and Queen of Montanari. They wouldn't like her. They wouldn't like her at all. She'd ruined the plan to unite the neighbouring kingdoms and was going to give Montanari an illegitimate heir. Her face was probably currently fixed to a dartboard or archery target in their throne room.

'And are they forcing you to do this too?' The words came out in a whisper. Every muscle in her body was tensed.

Duty. That was what she was sensing here.

He might be sincere. But there was no love—no compassion here. Tears threatened to fill her eyes. She licked her dry lips and stepped back, out of his hold. He hadn't answered her question and she couldn't quite believe how hurt she felt.

'I think you should go back to Montanari, Sebastian. I'll let you know when the baby arrives and we can sort things out from there.'

He looked surprised, his hand still in the air from where he'd touched her hair. He stared at it for a second, then shook his head. 'Who says I'm going back to Montanari?'

She concentrated on her shoes. It was easier than looking at him. 'Well, you will, won't you? You'll have—' she waved her hand '—princely duties or something to do. You can't stay here. There's been enough tittle-tattle about who the father of my baby is. The last thing I want is for someone to realise who you are and gossip about us. I'm the talk of the steamie already.'

He shook his head in bewilderment. 'The what?'

'The steamie. You know—the washhouse.'

He shook his head. 'I have no idea what you're talking about. But you know what? Just keep talking. I'd forgotten how much I loved the sound of your voice.'

Ditto.

'The steamie. It's a Scottish term for an old washhouse—the place where people used to go and wash their clothes before everyone had washing machines. It was notorious. The women used to always gossip in there.'

'So, that's what we could be? The talk of the steamie?'

She nodded again. 'And I'd rather not be. It would be easier if you left. We can talk. We can make plans about access arrangements when the baby arrives. We have another six weeks to wait. There's enough time.'

'Oh, no, you don't,' he replied promptly.

She had a bad feeling about this. 'What do you mean?'

'I'm not going anywhere. I've already missed out on things. I'm not missing out on anything else.'

'What do you mean by that?' she asked again.

He leaned against the door jamb and folded his arms across his chest. There was a determined grin on his face. 'I've got work to do here.' He mimicked her hand wave. 'Princely duties.

I need to sort out the twinning of our hospitals and iron out all the details. Get used to me being around.' He gave her a little nod. 'I'm your new best friend.'

CHAPTER THREE

IF HE DIDN'T love his friend so much he'd be annoyed by the permanent smile that seemed to have fixed itself to Oliver's face. Even sitting at a desk swamped with paperwork, Oliver still had the smile plastered on his face.

'Sebastian!' Oliver jumped to his feet, strode around the desk and engulfed Sebastian in a bear hug.

Sebastian returned the hug and leaned back. 'You're engaged? Do I get to meet the lucky lady?'

Oliver slapped his arm. 'You get to be my best man!' His smile wavered for a second. 'Are you here for the announcement tomorrow? I thought I would have heard from you.'

Sebastian gave a brief nod. He pushed his hands into his pockets and looked at Oliver. 'Not just that. It seems you and I are about to experience some changes together.'

Oliver's brow furrowed at the cryptic line. 'What do you mean?'

Sebastian glanced around. There was no one hovering near the door. Oliver's office seemed private enough. 'We're both about to be fathers.'

For a few seconds Oliver's expression was pure surprise. 'Theresa's pregnant? Congratulations. I had no idea—'

Sebastian held up his hand to stop him. Of course he was surprised. He knew Sebastian's real feelings about that engagement.

He shook his head. 'It's not Theresa.'

Oliver paled. 'It's not?'

They were good friends. He'd experienced Sebastian's parents. He knew exactly how focused and overbearing they could be. They'd spent many hours and a number of cases of beer contemplating the pressures of being an heir, along with Sebastian's personal feelings and ambitions.

The grin that spread over Oliver's face took Sebastian by surprise. He let out a laugh and walked back around the desk, pushing his wheeled chair back, putting his feet on the desk and crossing his arms. 'Oh, this is going to be good. Tell me all about it.'

Sebastian shook his head and leaned on the chair opposite Oliver. 'You find this amusing?'

Oliver nodded. 'I find this very amusing. It's only taken you thirty-one years to cause a scandal. I hope it's a good one.'

Sebastian made a face. 'You might change your mind when you find out the rest of it.'

'What's that supposed to mean?'

Sebastian shook his head again. 'Is everything set for the board meeting tomorrow?'

Oliver nodded. 'It's just a formality. They've already agreed to twin the hospitals and develop the training programme. You realise as soon as it's announced there'll be around forty staff queued outside my door trying to get their name on the reciprocal swap programme?'

Sebastian took a deep breath. Was there even a chance in a million that Sienna might consider something like that?

He was still smarting about her reaction earlier. What was wrong with making the heir to the Montanari throne legitimate? It made perfect sense to him.

Why was she so against it? He'd still felt the chemistry in the air between them—even if she wanted to deny it. He could admit that the timing wasn't great. But he'd dealt with things as best he could.

At the end of the day it was his duty to marry the mother of his baby. Maybe he could work on her, get her to reconsider?

'I plan on being around for the next few days—maybe longer.'

Oliver glanced at him. Sebastian's visits were usually only when he flew in and out of the UK on business and usually only lasted a couple of hours.

'Really, why?'

He'd picked up a pen and was scribbling notes.

Sebastian lowered his voice. 'Because I have to convince the mother of my child to marry me.'

The pen froze and oh-so-slowly one of Oliver's eyebrows rose. 'Say that again?'

Sebastian sat back in the chair and relaxed his arms back. He felt better after saying it out loud. It didn't seem quite so ridiculous a thought.

'Sienna—the mother of my child. I have to convince her to marry me.'

The pen flew past his ear. Oliver was on his feet. 'What? What do you mean, Sienna?' His head turned quickly from side to side. 'I mean, you? Her? The baby? It's yours?' It was almost as if he were trying to sort it all out in his mind. Then his eyes widened and he crumpled back down into his seat.

'Oh, no.' He looked as if he were going to be sick on the desk. 'How did you find out?' He didn't even wait for an answer. His head was already in his hands.

Sebastian gave a nod, reached over and clapped the side of one of Oliver's hands. 'Yep. It was you. You phoned about Ella and mentioned Sienna and how pregnant she was.'

Oliver's head shot back up. 'I thought you'd gone quiet when we spoke but I just assumed it was because you were surprised when I said Ella was pregnant.'

'It wasn't Ella's pregnancy that surprised me.'

Oliver ran his hand through his hair. 'Yeah, obviously.'

He wrinkled his nose and a smile broke out on his face. 'You and Sienna, really?'

Sebastian was curious. 'What's so strange about me and Sienna?'

Oliver threw up his hands. 'It's just...it's just...she's so... *Sienna*.' He shook his head and laughed. 'Your parents will hate her. She'd be their ultimate nightmare for a queen.'

Sebastian felt a little flare of protective anger. 'What's that supposed to mean?'

Oliver shrugged. 'Where will I start? She's a surgeon. She's *always* going to be a surgeon. Sienna would never give up her job—she's just too good and too emotionally connected. Surgery is in her blood.' He was shaking his head. 'As for tactfulness and decorum? Sienna's one of the most straight-talking doctors I've ever known. She doesn't take any prisoners. She wouldn't spend hours trying to butter up some foreign dignitary. She'd tell them exactly what she expected of them and then move on to dessert.' He tapped his fingers on the table and stared up to the left for a second. 'It's almost like you picked the person least like your mother in the whole world. Except for looks, of course. Your mother was probably born knowing she'd one day be Queen. I bet even as a child Sienna never played dress-up princesses or looked for a prince. She'd have been too busy setting up her dolls' hospital.'

Sebastian had been about to interrupt, instead he took a breath. Oliver had absolutely nailed it.

Sienna was a career woman. His mother had always taken a back seat to his father in every way.

Sienna hadn't been scared to shout at him. He'd never heard his mother raise her voice in her life.

Sienna hadn't been afraid to be bold and take him up on his proposition. Her comment *How about you listen to it all night instead?* had haunted his dreams in every erotic way possible. His mother would have a heart attack if she ever knew.

Just as well Sienna was a doctor really.

The reality of his future life was starting to crash all around him. Sebastian didn't panic. He'd never panicked. But he felt wary. If he didn't handle things well this could be a disaster.

Could Sienna McDonald really be the future Queen of Montanari?

He leaned back and folded his arms. 'She's the mother of my child. Montanari needs an heir. It's my duty to marry her.'

Oliver raised his eyebrows. 'Please tell me you didn't just say that?'

When Sebastian didn't answer right away, Oliver shook his head. 'More importantly, please tell me you didn't say that to Sienna?'

Sebastian ignored the comment. 'Montanari needs change. Sienna will be just the breath of fresh air it needs. Who couldn't love her? She's a neonatal surgeon. She eats, breathes and sleeps her job. People will admire her intelligence. They'll admire her dedication. I know I do.'

Oliver started tapping his fingers on the table again. 'And what does Sienna have to say about all this?'

He was good. He was too good. He clearly knew Sienna well.

'Let's just say that Sienna and I are a work in progress.'

Oliver let out something resembling a snort. He stood up again. 'You're my oldest friend, Sebastian, but I'm telling you right now, I'm not choosing sides. She's one of my best doctors. Upset her and you'll upset me.' He gave a little shudder. 'She'll kill me when she finds out it was me that told you.' He leaned against the wall for a second. 'Why didn't she tell you herself?'

Sebastian shrugged slightly. 'Timing, she says. I'd just got engaged.'

Oliver rolled his eyes then narrowed them again. 'And why didn't you tell me that you'd got in a compromising position with one of my doctors?' He wagged his finger at Sebastian. 'Can't trust you for two minutes. I'll need to rethink this whole hospital-twinning thing. Can't have us sending all our doctors over there to get seduced by Montanari men—royal or not.'

Sebastian stood up. 'I have a baby on the way. My priorities have changed.' He headed to the door. 'I'll see you at the board meeting tomorrow—and for the press announcement.'

Oliver gave a nod. He tipped his head to one side. 'So, what's your next plan?'

Sebastian shot him a wide smile. 'Charm. Why else be a prince?'

Sienna stuck her head outside the doors to the paediatric ICU, then ducked back inside, keeping her nose pressed against the glass. The tinsel taped to the window tickled her nose and partially blocked her view.

'What are you doing?' asked an amused Charlie Warren, one of her OBGYN colleagues.

'I'd have thought that was clear. I'm hiding.' Her ever-expanding belly was stopping her from getting a clear view.

Charlie laughed. 'And who are you hiding from?'

'You know. Him.'

'Him, who?'

Sienna sighed and turned around, leaning back against the door.

'Sebastian.'

Charlie nodded slowly. 'Ah…now I see.'

Sienna brushed a lock of loose hair out of her eyes. 'I see the Teddy's super-speed grapevine is working as well as ever. He's been here less than twenty-four hours.'

Charlie leaned against the door with her and gave her a knowing smile.

'What are you grinning at?' she half snapped.

She'd always liked Charlie. They got on well. All her colleagues had been so supportive of her pregnancy. She stared at him again.

'There's something different about you.'

'There is? What?' He had a dopey kind of grin on his face.

She pointed. 'That. You've got the same look that Oliver is wearing.'

'I don't know what you mean.'

She poked her finger in his chest. 'Oh, yes, you do. What's her name?'

She was definitely curious. She'd spent the last week so wrapped up with preparations for Christmas and trying to keep her energy up that she'd obviously missed something important. Charlie was a widower. For as long as she'd known him there had been veiled shadows behind his eyes.

They were gone now. And it made her heart sing a little to see that.

He gave her a sheepish smile. 'It's Juliet.'

Sienna's mouth dropped open. 'No.' Then she couldn't help but grin. 'Really?' She got on well with the Aussie surgeon who'd performed *in-utero* surgery to save the life of a quad born at Teddy's last week.

His smile said it all. 'Really.'

She leaned against the door again. 'Oh, wow.' She flicked her hair back. It was really beginning to annoy her. 'First Oliver and now you. Lovesick people are falling all over the place.' She gave him a wicked glare. 'Better phone Public Health, it looks like we've got an infectious disease here.'

He nodded. 'Don't forget Max and Annabelle. This thing is spreading faster than that winter virus.' He gave her a cheeky wink. 'And from what I saw this morning at breakfast, others might eventually succumb.'

Heat rushed into her cheeks. She'd come in early this morning and walked along to the canteen for breakfast. She'd barely sat down before

Sebastian had ambushed her and sat down at the other side of the table with coffee, toast and eggs.

It had been excruciating. She could sense every eye in the canteen on them both and it had been as quick as she could bolt down her porridge and hurry out of there.

Normally she loved breakfast in the canteen at Christmas time. Christmas pop tunes were always playing and the menu food got new names like Rudolph's raisin pancakes or Santa's scrumptious scrambled egg.

'I don't know what you mean,' she said defensively to Charlie, who was obviously trying to wind her up.

He laughed as he pulled open the door and looked out for a second. 'He seems like a nice guy. Maybe you should give him a chance.'

She laid her hand on her large stomach. 'Oh, I think it's pretty obvious I've already given him a chance.'

He just kept laughing. 'Well, he's on the charm offensive. And he's winning. Everyone that's met him thinks he's one version of wonderful or another. Including Juliet's daughter.'

'He's met her daughter?'

Charlie nodded. 'She loves him already. He

gave her some kind of doll that the little girls in Montanari love. A special Christmas one with a red and green dress. She was over the moon.'

Sienna wrinkled her nose. 'You shouldn't let her speak to strangers.'

Something flashed over Charlie's face. 'If I didn't know any better, Sienna, I'd think you were a woman reaching that crabby stage just before she delivers.'

She shook her head fiercely and patted her stomach. 'Oh, no. No way. I've got just under six weeks. This baby is not coming out before then.'

'If you say so.' Charlie stuck his head out of the door again. 'Okay, you can go. The coast is clear. Just remember to be on your best behaviour.' He held the door before her as she rushed outside. 'And just remember... I recognise the signs.'

The coast wasn't clear at all.

Sebastian was waiting outside the unit, leaning against the wall with his arms folded.

'I'm going to kill Charlie with my bare hands,' she muttered.

It didn't help that he was looking even sexier than before. When he'd joined her this morning at breakfast he'd been wearing a suit and tie.

Something to do with a business meeting. She hadn't really been paying attention.

Now, he'd changed into jeans, a leather jacket and a slim-fitting black T-shirt. His hair was speckled with flecks of snow.

'What are you doing here?' she asked as she made her best attempt to sweep past.

Sebastian was having none of it. He fell into step beside her. 'Waiting for you.'

She stopped walking and turned to face him. She wanted to be angry with him. She wanted to be annoyed. But he had that look on his face, that hint of cheek. He was deliberately taunting her. They'd spent most of the weekend in Montanari batting smart comments back and forth. This felt more like sun-blessed Montanari than the snow-dusted Cotswolds.

She stifled her smile. 'This better not get to be a habit. I'm busy, Seb. I'm at work.'

His grin broadened and she realised her error. She'd called him Seb again.

'When do you finish work?'

'Why?'

'You know why. I'd like us to talk—have dinner maybe. Do something together.'

His phone buzzed in his pocket. He shifted a little on his feet but ignored it.

'Aren't you going to get that?'

He shook his head. 'I'm busy.'

'How long—exactly—have you been standing out here?'

He smiled. 'Around two hours.' He lifted one hand and shrugged. 'But it's fine. The people around here are very friendly. They all like to talk.'

'Talk is exactly what they'll do. You might be a public figure, Seb, but I'm not. I'm a pretty private person. I don't want anyone else knowing about our baby.'

The look on his face was so surprised that she realised he hadn't even considered that.

How far apart were they? Had he not even considered that might put her under stress? Not exactly ideal for a pregnant woman.

And it didn't help that wherever Seb was, men in black were permanently hovering in the background.

He'd already made the assumption that she would want to marry him. Maybe he also thought she would be fine about having their baby in the public eye?

Oh, no.

She gave a sway.

'Sienna? What's wrong? Are you okay?'

He moved right in front of her, catching both her arms with his firm hands. He was close enough for her to see the tiny lines around his eyes and the little flecks in his forest-green eyes.

'You're a prince,' she breathed slowly.

He blinked. There was a look of amusement on his face. 'I'm a prince,' he confirmed in a whisper.

'I slept with a prince.' It was almost as if she were talking to herself. She knew all this. None of it was a surprise. But all of a sudden things were sinking in fast.

Before, Sebastian Falco hadn't featured in her life. Apart from the telltale parting gift that he'd left her, there was really no sign of any connection between them. No one knew about their weekend together. No one knew that they'd even met.

When she'd come back, it was clear that even though Oliver was Sebastian's friend, he'd had no idea about their relationship.

That was the way things were supposed to be. Even though, in her head, she'd known she should tell Seb about the baby, once the engagement was announced she'd pushed those thoughts away.

She'd pushed all memories of Sebastian and their time together—the touch of his hands on her skin, the taste of his lips on hers—away into that castle of his that she'd never seen.

A castle. The man lived in a castle. Not in the mountain retreat he'd taken her to. Her stomach gave a little flip as she wondered once more how many other women had been there.

'Sienna, honey? Are you okay? Do you want to sit down?'

Honey. He'd just called her honey as if it were the most natural thing in the world to do.

He wanted them to get married. A prince wanted to marry her.

Most women would be happy. Most women would be delighted.

Marry a prince. Live in a castle. Wasn't that the basis of every little girl's favourite fairy tale?

Not hers.

She wasn't a Cinderella kind of girl. Well, maybe just a little bit.

She definitely wasn't Rapunzel. She didn't need any guy to save her.

And she so wasn't Sleeping Beauty. She'd never spend her life lying about.

She looked around. They were three floors up. The glass atrium dome above them and the Christmas decorations directly underneath them. People flowed all around them. The Royal Cheltenham Hospital was world renowned. People begged to work here. Posts were fiercely contested. Three other surgeons she respected and admired had interviewed for the job that she'd been appointed to.

That had been the best call of her life.

She sucked in a breath. Teddy's was her life.

She loved her job, loved the kids, loved the surgeries and loved the people.

A gust of icy wind blew up through the open doors downstairs. The chill felt appropriate.

The kids' book character in front of her right now was threatening all that.

Would she really get any peace once people found out her child was the heir of Montanari?

Her hands went protectively to her stomach. 'What happens once he or she arrives?'

He looked confused. 'What do you mean?'

So much was spinning around in her head that the words stuck in her throat. After her childhood experiences she'd always vowed to be in charge of her own life, her own relationships and her own destiny.

Finding out she was pregnant had only made her sway for a second or two, then it had just put a new edge to her determination to get things right.

She'd made so many plans this Christmas—almost as if she were trying to keep herself busy. Carolling. Helping on the children's ward. Wrapping presents for army troops stationed away from home. Oh, her house was decorated as usual, and she opened the doors on her advent calendar every day. But she'd pictured spending this Christmas alone so was scheduled to be working over the holiday. She hadn't counted on Sebastian being around.

Seb was still standing straight in front of her, looking at her with concern in his eyes. He reached up and brushed her cheek with the gentlest of touches—the most tender of touches. It sent a whole host of memories flooding through her.

Seb. The man she'd shared a bed with. The man who kissed like no other. The man she'd thought was someone else entirely.

The man who'd thought he could walk in here and sweep her off her feet.

She shivered. She actually shivered.

'What are the rules in Montanari? Did you propose to me because an illegitimate child can't inherit the throne?'

He shook his head. 'No. No, of course I didn't. And no. There's no rules like that in Montanari. I'm the heir to the throne, and my firstborn son, or firstborn daughter, will be the heir to the throne once I'm King.' He gave an almost indiscernible shake of his head. 'But let's face it, it would be much better if we were married.'

'Better for who?'

He held up his hands, but she wasn't watching his hands, she was watching his face.

'Better for everyone. I have a duty—a duty to my people and my country. I want to introduce our son or daughter as the heir to the throne.' His gaze softened. 'And I'd like to introduce you as my wife.'

She had an instant dual flashback. One part caused by his word 'duty'. An instant memory of just exactly how both her parents had felt about their 'duty' and the look of absolute relief on her father's face as he'd packed his bags and left. The second part was caused by the first. A memory from months ago—those first few weeks when apparent morning sickness had struck at any second of the day or night. She wanted to be sick right here, right now. Right over his brown boots.

Duty. A word that seemed to have an absolute chilling effect that penetrated right down to her soul. Every time she heard people use the word in everyday life she had to try and hold back her instant response—an involuntary shudder.

Her insides were curled in knots. He'd just told her he wanted to marry her—again.

But not for the right reasons.

It didn't matter that her back had ached these last few days, she drew herself up to her full height and looked him straight in the eye.

It was almost like putting blinkers on. She wouldn't let those forest-green eyes affect her in the way they had before.

'I have a duty. To myself and to my child. We aren't your duty. We belong to ourselves. No one else. Not you. Not your parents. Not your people. I spent my childhood watching two people who should have never got together barely tolerate each other.' Fire was starting to burn inside her.

'What did you get for your eighteenth birthday present, Sebastian?'

The question caught him unawares. He stumbled around for the answer. 'A car, I think. Or a watch.'

'Well, good for you. Do you know what I got? I got my father packing his bags and leaving. But that didn't hurt nearly as much as the look of complete relief on his face. As for my mother? Two months later she moved to Portugal and found herself a toy boy. I can honestly say I've never seen her happier.' She pressed her hand to her chest. 'I did that to them, Sebastian. I made two people who shouldn't have been together spend eighteen years in what must have been purgatory for them.' She shook her head fiercely. 'I will never, *ever* do that to a child of mine.'

Sebastian pulled back. He actually pulled back a little.

She'd done it again. Twice, in the space of two days, she'd raised her voice to Sebastian in a public place. Perfect. The talk of the steamie again.

But she couldn't help it. She wasn't finished.

There was no way Mr Fancy-Watches-For-His-Birthday could sweep in here and be part of her and her baby's life.

While she might have had a few little day dreams about the guy who was engaged to someone else, her reality plans had been way, way different.

This was why she'd negotiated new hours for the job she loved. This was why she'd visited four different nurseries and interviewed six potential childminders. This was why she'd spoken to her friend Bonnie—a fellow Scot who'd transported to Cambridge—on a number of occasions about how best to handle being a single mum.

This man was messing with her mind. Messing with her plans.

She didn't need this now. She really didn't.

She held up her hand. She knew exactly how to get rid of him. And not a single word would be a lie.

'I don't want this, Sebastian. This isn't my life. This isn't my dream. I will never, ever marry a man out of duty.' She almost spat out the word.

She lifted her hands towards the snow-topped atrium. 'When, and if, I ever get married, I'll get married to the man I love with all my heart. The man I couldn't bear to spend a single day without in my life. The man who would walk in front of a speeding train for me or my child without a single thought for himself—just like I would for him.' She took a few steps away from him. She was aware that a few people had stopped conversations around them to listen but she was past the point of caring.

'You don't know me, Sebastian. I want the whole hog. I want everything. And this, what you're offering? It doesn't even come close. I want a man who loves and adores me, who will walk by my side no matter what direction I take. I want a man who can take my breath away with a single look, a single touch.'

She could see him flinch. It didn't matter she was being unfair. Sebastian had taken more than her breath away with his looks and touches, but he didn't need to know that, not right now.

'I want a husband who will be proud of me and my career. Who won't care that I'm on call and he might need to reorganise his life around me. Who'll help around the house and not expect a wife who'll cook him dinner. Public Health may well have to do investigations into my cooking skills.'

She was enjoying herself now, taking it too far. But he had to know. He had to know just how fast to run.

'I will never accept anything less. I've been the child of a duty marriage. I would never, ever do that to my child. It's a form of torture. Growing up feeling guilty? It's awful.' She pressed her hands on her stomach again. '*My* child—' she emphasised the word '—is going to grow up feeling loved, blessed and, above all, wanted. By me, at least. There will be rules. There will be discipline. But most of all, there will be love.'

She walked back up to stand right in front of him. 'Whoever loves me will know how much I love Christmas, will want to celebrate it with me every year. Will know the songs I love, the crazy carols I love to sing. They won't care that I spend hours wrapping presents that are opened in seconds, they won't care that I buy more Christmas decorations than there is space for on the tree, they won't care that I have to have a special kind of cake every Christmas Eve and spend a fortune trying to find it. They'll know that I would only ever get married at Christmas. They would never even suggest anything else.'

She took a deep breath and finally looked at him—really looked at him.

Yip, she'd done it. He looked as if she'd just run over him with an Edinburgh tram. This time she lowered her voice. 'You might be a prince. You might have a castle. But I want the fairy tale. And you can't give it to me.'

And with that, she turned and walked away.

CHAPTER FOUR

'ARE YOU COMING down with something?' Oliver was staring at him in a way only a doctor could.

'What? No. Don't be ridiculous.'

Oliver gave a slow, careful nod. 'The board paper was excellent. They love the idea. It looks like the Falco charm has done its magic.'

'Except where it counts.'

'What's that supposed to mean?' Oliver rolled his eyes. 'No. Please. I'm not sure I want to know.' He walked around the desk and leaned against the wall.

Sebastian sighed loudly. He couldn't help it. 'I thought once I came here, Sienna might be happy to see me again. I didn't expect her to be quite...quite...'

'Quite so Sienna?' Oliver was looking far too amused for his liking.

Sebastian let out a wry laugh. 'Yeah, exactly. Quite so Sienna. I still can't believe she didn't let me know.'

Oliver shook his head. 'Doesn't sound like her. She's fierce. She's independent. She's stubborn—'

'You're not helping.'

Oliver laughed. 'But she's also one of the kindest-hearted women I know. She's always been professional but I can't tell you how many times I've caught her sobbing in a dark corner somewhere when things aren't going well with one of her patients. Working with neonates is the toughest area for any doctor. They're just getting started at life. They deserve a chance. And Sienna needs to be tough to get through it. She needs to be determined.' He paused for a second and his steady gaze met Sebastian's. 'Sienna puts up walls. She's honest. She's loyal. If she didn't let you know about the baby—she must have had a darn good reason.'

Sebastian bit the inside of his cheek. All of Oliver's words were striking chords with him. 'She said it was the engagement announcement. It put her off. She didn't want to destroy my engagement and cause a scandal.'

Oliver's brow creased. 'That's very considerate of her.' He stood up straight and took a few steps towards Sebastian. 'Quick question, Seb. Did you believe that?'

Sebastian was surprised. It hadn't occurred to him to doubt what Sienna told him. 'What do you mean?'

Oliver started shaking his head. 'I guess I just think it could be something else.'

'What do you mean?'

Oliver began walking around. 'It all sounds very noble. But would Sienna really deny you the chance to know your child? She could have spoken to me—she knows we are friends—I could have found a way to get a discreet message to you.' He gave Sebastian a careful look. 'I wonder if there was something else—a different kind of reason.'

Sebastian shifted in his chair. He couldn't get his head around what Oliver was saying. 'What do you mean? You think the baby might not be mine?'

Oliver held up his hand. 'Oh, no. Sienna wasn't seeing anyone. I couldn't even tell you when she had her last date. She's totally dedicated to her work. You don't need to worry about that.'

Thoughts started swirling around his head as relief flooded through him. Sienna had nailed exactly why he had come here. Duty. That was how he always lived his life.

It had been instilled in him from the youngest age.

He might not have loved Theresa. But she would have fulfilled the role of Queen with grace and dignity.

Sienna? Her personality type was completely different. She was intelligent. She was a brilliant surgeon. But she hadn't been brought up in a royal family. She didn't know traditions and protocols. He wasn't entirely sure she would ever follow them or want to.

He was pushing aside the way his heart skipped a beat when he saw her. The way his body reacted instantly. Passion like that would never last a lifetime no matter how pleasurable.

But that passion had created the baby currently residing inside Sienna. His baby. The heir to the throne of Montanari.

He stared back at Oliver. Knowing there were no other men in Sienna's life was exactly what he needed to hear. His press team were already wondering how to handle the imminent announcement about the baby.

'Then what on earth are you talking about?'

He was getting increasingly frustrated by Oliver talking around in circles.

Oliver ran his hand through his hair. 'Let's just say I recognise the signs.'

'The signs of what? By the time you actually tell me what you mean this baby will be an adult.'

Oliver laughed again and started counting off on his fingers. 'Do you know what I've noticed in the last day? Sienna's twitchy. She's on edge. She's different. Throughout this whole pregnancy she's been as cool as a cucumber.'

'You think I'm having a bad effect on her?'

Oliver put his hand on Sebastian's arm. 'I think you're having *some* kind of effect on her. I've never seen her like this.' He gave a little smile. 'If I didn't know any better—I'd say Sienna McDonald likes you a whole lot more than she admits to.'

Sebastian was stunned. 'Really?'

Oliver raised his eyebrows. 'It's such an alien concept to you?'

A warm feeling spread all over Sebastian's skin, as if the sun had penetrated through his shirt and annihilated the winter chill. When he'd proposed marriage the other day it had been an automatic reaction—something he'd planned on the flight over. But it had been precipitated by duty. Their baby would be the heir to the throne in Montanari.

Part of him was worried. She did actually like him? Was that why Sienna was acting the way she did?

He stood up and started pacing. 'She told me outright she'd never marry me. She told me she wanted everything. Love, romance, marriage, a husband who would love and adore her. She told me being a prince wasn't enough—not nearly enough.'

'And you thought it would be?' Oliver's face said it all. 'How come I've known you all these years and never realised how stupid you were?'

He stood up, stepped forward and poked his finger into Sebastian's chest. 'How do you feel about Sienna? How do you feel about her in here?'

His answer came out automatically. 'What does that matter? A marriage in Montanari is usually about a union. On this occasion, it's about a child. Feelings don't come into it.'

It was an uncomfortable question. Memories of Sienna McDonald had swirled around his head for months. The most obscure thing—a smell, a word—could conjure Sienna front and foremost in his mind again. The briefest thought could send blood rushing all around his body. His first sight of her—pregnant with his child—had affected him in ways he hadn't even contemplated.

From the second he'd met her Sienna had got under his skin.

The sight of her, the taste of her, the smell of her was irresistible. The way she responded to his teasing. He did care about her. He did care about this baby. But could it be more?

How would someone like him know what love was anyway? It wasn't as if he'd spent a life exposed to it. He'd had teenage crushes. A few passionate flings. But marrying for love had never really been on his radar. Sienna's words and expectations the other day had taken him by surprise.

Oliver folded his arms and raised his eyebrows. He knew Sebastian far too well to take his glib answer at face value.

'I...I...I...' He threw up his hands in frustration. 'I don't know. She confuses me. I never contemplated having emotional ties to the woman I'd marry. Sienna has just mixed everything up.'

Oliver shook his head. 'Then hurry up and decide. Hurry up and decide how you feel about the mother of your child. A beautiful, headstrong and highly intelligent member of my staff *and* a friend of mine.' He took a step closer and held up his finger and thumb almost pressed together. 'Do you want to know how much Sienna McDonald will care about you being a prince? Do you want to know how much a palace will impress her? This much.'

Oliver walked away and sat down behind his desk. He looked at Sebastian carefully. 'The trouble with you is that you've had too much help in this life.'

'What's that supposed to mean?'

Oliver waved his hand. 'Someone to do this for you, someone to do that. You didn't even do your own grocery shopping when we were students together.'

Sebastian looked embarrassed.

'Sienna doesn't have that. Sienna has never had that. Everything for this baby, she's worked out for herself. She's juggled her schedule. Worked out her maternity leave to the second. Put plans in place for every patient.' He put his elbows on the desk. 'Everything to do with her house— what we'd call a fixer-upper—she's sorted out herself too. She's spent years saving to get the house she really wants. It's not a house to her—it's a home. Do you know how crazy she is about Christmas? Do you know that she's a fabulous baker?' Oliver sighed.

Sebastian shook his head. 'All I know about Sienna is what I learned on that weekend back in Montanari, and what I've learned in the last few days. Everything's a mess. She's still angry with me—angry that I was engaged to someone else. She told me exactly what she wanted in this life and it was the whole fairy tale.' He dropped his voice slightly. 'She also told me I wasn't part of it. I have no idea how to connect with this woman, Oliver. I have no idea how I can manage to persuade her to give the thought of us a chance. Sometimes I think she doesn't even like me.'

Oliver frowned. 'Oh, she likes you—I can tell.'

'She does?' It was the first thing that gave him some hope.

Oliver leaned back again and looked his friend up and down as if he were assessing him. 'In the past she's been very selective. Guys who don't live up to her expectations?' He snapped his fingers and gave Sebastian a wicked grin. 'Gone. Just like that.'

Sebastian had started to feel uncomfortable.

But Oliver was his friend—he couldn't keep up his serious face for long. It was obvious he cared about the welfare of Sienna. And Sebastian was glad about that, glad to know that people had her back.

He folded his arms across his chest and leaned against the wall. Some of the things that Oliver had said had struck a chord. There were so many things about Sienna that he didn't know. Things he wanted to know.

The bottom line was—could Sienna really be Queen material?

One weekend was not enough. It would never be enough. But he wasn't sure he wanted to say that out loud now. At least not to his friend.

'So, how do I get to know the real Sienna McDonald—the one behind the white coat?'

Oliver smiled. 'Eh, I think you've already achieved that.' He raised his eyebrow. 'There is evidence.'

Sebastian started pacing. Things were rushing around in his mind. 'Stop it. What about the other stuff? The Christmas stuff? What she takes in her tea?' His footsteps slowed. 'How she wants to raise our kid?' His voice got quieter. 'If she actually might more than like me…'

He stopped. Sienna. He needed to be around Sienna.

Oliver gave him a smile. 'I guess you should go and find out.'

It was an Aston Martin DB5. She'd seen one in a James Bond movie once. Even she could recognise it. A classic machine. She should have known he'd own something like this. He opened the door of the pale blue car revealing a red leather interior and she sucked in her breath.

She'd never been a show-me-your-money-and-I'll-be-impressed kind of girl. But this was a bit different. This was pure class. She'd watched enough car shows in her time to know that owning a car like this was a labour of pure love.

Just looking at it made her tingle.

The streets were dusted with snow. People were crossing the car park and staring, nudging each other and pointing at the car.

Christmas lights lit up the street opposite. Every shop had decorations in its windows. She could hear Christmas pop songs drifting out of the pub across the road. At the end of the road was a courtyard where a giant tree was lit with gold and red lights. It was paid for by the local council and the kids on the paediatric ward could see it from their windows. The lights twinkled all night long.

'What are you doing, Sebastian?'

He smiled. He was dressed for the British weather in a pair of jeans, black boots and his black leather jacket. She gave a little gulp as her insides did some weird little flip-flop.

He smiled. Oh, no. The flip-flop turned into a somersault. 'I came to pick you up. Someone told me you had car trouble. I thought I could drive you home.'

She bit her lip. Tempting. Oh, so tempting.

'I can call for roadside assistance. I really need to get my car sorted. It shouldn't take too long.'

He waved his hand. 'Albie, the porter, said if you leave your keys with him he'll get your car started later. It's too cold to hang around and wait for roadside assistance.' He stepped a little closer.

There it was. That familiar aroma. The one that took her back to Montanari, and sun, and cocktails, and…

'We could pick up a little dinner on the way home.'

Her stomach let out a loud growl. It was almost as if her body were conspiring against her. She scrambled to find a suitable excuse but her stubborn brain remained blank. 'Well, I...I...'

'Great. That's sorted, then.' He took her car keys from her hand and walked swiftly back to the hospital, leaving her to stare at the pale blue machine in front of her, gleaming as the sun dipped lower in the sky.

She was still staring a few seconds later when he returned. He stood alongside her and smiled. 'Like it?'

She couldn't help the smile as she met his proud gaze. 'I guess I'm just a little surprised.'

'By what?'

She waved her hand towards the car. 'I guess I thought you might be in something sleek, low-slung and bright red.'

He laughed out loud. 'You think I'm one of *those* kind of guys?'

She nearly laughed herself. He really didn't need to elaborate. But as she kept staring at the car she felt a wave of something else. 'I guess I don't really know, do I?'

She turned to look at him, her warm breath frosting the air between them. Those dark green eyes seemed even more intense in the darkening light. He held her gaze. She could see his chest rise and fall as he watched her, searching her face.

All of a sudden she felt a little self-conscious. Was there any make-up even left on her skin? When was the last time she'd combed her hair?

This time Sebastian wasn't smiling. He was looking at her in a way she couldn't really fathom. As if there were a thousand thoughts spinning around in his head.

He would be King one day. He would be King of his country. She'd tried not to think about any of this. It had been easy before. He was engaged. He was getting married. He was with someone else.

But now he was here.

Here, in the Cotswolds, to see her. Her, and their baby.

He leaned forward and she held her breath, wondering what would happen next.

His arm brushed against hers as he pulled open the car door. 'Then let's do something about that,' he said huskily.

Snowflakes started to fall around her. She looked up at the now dark purple streaked sky. She could almost swear that there was something sparkling in the air between them.

As she took a step towards the car he turned towards her again, his arm settling at the side of her waist.

'In case you haven't noticed, I'm not a flashy kind of guy. I like classics. Things that will last a lifetime. Something that every time you look at it, it makes your heart flutter just a little. Because you know it's a keeper. You know it was made just for you.'

She couldn't breathe. She couldn't actually breathe. Large snowflakes were landing on his head and shoulders. His warm breath touched her cheek as he spoke—he was that close. Her hand rose automatically, resting on his arm. They were face to face. Almost cheek to cheek. If she tilted her chin up just a little...

But she couldn't. Not yet. Maybe not ever. She needed her head to be clear around Sebastian. And right now it was anything but clear.

It was full of intense green eyes framed by dark lashes, a sexy smile and sun-kissed skin. She could smell the leather of his jacket mingling with the familiar scent of his aftershave. She could see the faint shadow along his jaw line. The palm of her hand itched to reach up and touch it.

She hadn't moved. And he hadn't moved either. Being this close was almost hypnotic.

But she had to. She had to look away. She broke his gaze and glanced back at the car. 'It's blue,' she said. 'I thought all these cars were silver.'

Cars. A safe topic. A neutral topic. Something that would stop the swell of emotion currently rising in her chest.

He blinked. His hand hadn't moved from her currently non-existent waist. He gave a nod. 'A lot of them were silver. James Bond's was silver. But mine? Mine is Caribbean blue. As soon as I saw it, and the red leather interior, I knew it was perfect. I had to have it.'

He held her gaze again and she licked her lips anxiously. *I had to have it* echoed in her head. Why did it feel as if he wasn't talking about the car?

There was a screech behind them. A bang. A huge shattering of glass. And they both jumped apart.

Two seconds later the air was filled by a blood-curdling scream.

Sebastian didn't hesitate. He ran instantly to-wards the scream.

The doctor's instinct in her surged forward. She

glanced towards the hospital doors. She could go and ask for help but Teddy's only took maternity and paediatric emergencies. It wasn't a district general and she didn't even know what was wrong yet.

She started running. Running wasn't easy at her current state of pregnancy. The ground was slippery beneath her feet as snow was just starting to settle on the ground.

As she reached the road that ran alongside the hospital she could see immediately what was wrong. One car had skidded and hit a lamp post. Another car had mounted the pavement and was now embedded in the dress shop's window. The Christmas decorations that had decorated the window were scattered across the street. She winced as her foot crunched on a red bauble. Sebastian was trying to talk to the woman who was screaming. He had his hands on both of her shoulders and was trying to calm her down.

Sienna's eyes swept over the scene, trying to make sense of the situation. An air bag had exploded in the car that had hit the lamp post. A young woman was currently slumped against it.

The other driver was slumped too. But there was no airbag. It was an older car and his head and shoulders were over the steering wheel of the car. The windscreen was shattered and shards of glass from the shop's window frame were directly above him.

The woman on the pavement was obviously in shock. She'd stopped screaming and was talking nonstop between sobs to Sebastian.

He turned towards her, his eyes wide. 'Her kid. Her kid is under the car.'

Another bystander stepped forward and put his arm around the woman, nodding towards Sebastian and Sienna. 'I've phoned an ambulance.'

Sienna gulped. She was familiar with obstetric emergencies. She was often called in for a consult if there could be an issue with the baby. Paediatric emergencies took up half of all her days. Neonates had a tendency to become very sick, very quickly and she needed to be available.

But regular emergencies?

She dropped to her knees and peered under the car. There was a mangled pushchair, and further away, out of her reach, a little figure.

Her heart leapt. Sebastian dropped down next to her, his head brushing against hers as he looked under the car.

He pressed his hand over hers. It was the quickest movement. The warmth of his hand barely had time to make an impact on her. 'I'll go.'

She hardly had time to speak before Sebastian was wriggling his way under the car. She opened her mouth to object just as baby gave her an almighty kick. Her hand went automatically to her belly. Of course. There was no way she could possibly fit under the body of the car—Sebastian was already struggling.

She edged around the front of the vehicle, watching the precarious shards of glass hanging above the car and staying on the ground as low as she could. The slush on the ground soaked her knees and legs, her cream winter coat attracting grime that would never be removed. She slid her arms out of the coat and pulled it over her head— at least she'd have some protection if glass fell.

'Can you try and feel for a pulse?' she said quietly to Sebastian, then added, 'Do you know what to do?'

There was a flicker of light. Sebastian had wriggled his phone from his pocket and turned on the torch, lying it on the ground next to him.

In amongst the darkness and wetness, Sienna thought she could spot something else. The little boy was still tangled in part of the buggy and her view was still partially obscured.

She turned to the people behind her. 'Can someone find out the little boy's name for me, please?'

Sebastian's face was grim; he had a hand up next to the little boy's head. 'Yes, I've got a pulse. It's fast and it feels faint.'

Truth was, so did she.

She nodded. 'What position is he in?'

Right now she so wished she could be under there. Her frustration at not being able to get to the child was building by the second.

'He's on his back. Wait.'

She couldn't see what Sebastian was doing. He was moving his hand and holding up the torch to the little guy's face.

A voice in her ear nearly made her jump out of her skin. 'Gabriel. The little boy's name is Gabriel.'

She sucked in a breath. 'Sebastian, tell me what's wrong. What can you see? His name is Gabriel. Is he conscious?'

The wait must only have been a few seconds but it felt like so much longer.

Sebastian's face was serious. He held up one

hand, palm facing towards her, and held his phone with the other so she could see. It was stained red.

'There's blood, Sienna. Lots of it. He's pale but there's something else—his lips are going a funny colour.'

Sienna turned to the crowd again, searching for the man's face she'd seen earlier. 'Any news about the ambulance?'

The man shook his head. 'Someone has run over to the hospital to try and get more help and some supplies.'

She nodded. 'I need swabs. Bandages. Oxygen. A finger monitor if they've got one.'

'I'll go,' said a young woman and ran off towards the hospital entrance.

Sienna felt in her pocket. All she had was an unopened packet of tissues. Not exactly the ideal product—but at least they were clean.

She threw them towards Sebastian. 'It's all I've got. Try and stem the flow of blood. Where is it coming from?'

Sebastian moved his body, blocking her view again, and she almost whimpered in frustration. She felt useless here. Absolutely useless. She couldn't check the child properly, assess any injuries or provide any care. It was the only time in her life she'd regretted being pregnant.

But Sebastian was calm. He wasn't panicking. He hadn't hesitated to slip under the car and help in any way that he could. As she watched he tore open the packet of tissues and tried to stem the flow of blood.

'It's coming from the side of his neck. I think he's been hit by some of the glass.' He paused for a second and she instantly knew something was wrong.

'What is it? Tell me?'

Sebastian kept his voice low. 'His lips are blue, Sienna.'

She hated this. She hated feeling helpless. 'Do you know what the recovery position is? Turn him on his side, Seb. Open his mouth and try and clear his airway. Check there's nothing inside his mouth. He's not getting enough oxygen into his lungs.'

The noise around them was increasing. There was a faint wail of sirens in the distance. The volume of the murmuring voices was increasing. People were always drawn to the scene of an accident. She could hear someone shouting instructions. A voice with some authority attached to it.

She could only pray it was a member of the hospital staff dealing with one of the drivers.

The driver. She should really look at him too. But her first priority was this child. If Gabriel didn't breathe he would be dead. If his airway was obstructed he would be dead. She had no idea the extent of his other injuries but no oxygen would certainly kill him. If she had a team around her right now they would take time to stabilise the little guy's head and neck. But she didn't have a team—and there wasn't time.

All she had was Sebastian—the Prince from another country who was under there trying to be her right-hand man.

She could hear him talking to the little boy, coaxing him, trying to see if he could get any response. Shadows were shifting under the car; it was still difficult to see what was going on.

'Sebastian? Have you stopped the bleeding? What about his colour? Have you managed to put him in the recovery position yet?'

'Give me a minute.' The voice was firm and steady.

He doesn't have a minute. She had to bite her tongue to stop herself from saying it out loud.

There was a clatter beside her. 'Sorry,' breathed a young woman. 'More help is coming.'

Sienna looked at the ground. There was a plastic tray loaded with supplies. She grabbed for the pulse oximeter. It was one of the simplest pieces of equipment they had—a simple little rubber pouch with a sensor that fitted over a finger and gave you an indication of someone's oxygen levels. She switched it on and reached as far under the car as she should, touching Sebastian's back.

'Here. Take this. Put it over his finger and tell me what the number is.'

Sebastian's position shifted. 'Come on, Gabriel,' he was saying encouragingly. He'd moved his torch. It was right at Gabriel's face, which was now facing away from her. For the briefest second she could see Sebastian's face reflected in the glass. He was focused. Concern and anxiety written all over his face.

She held her breath. His hand reached behind him to grab hold of the monitor. He'd heard her. He was just focusing on Gabriel.

She could almost swear her heart squeezed. If she were under the car right now, that was exactly how she'd be.

Focused on Gabriel. Not on any of the noise or circumstances around them.

'Watch out!' came the shout from her side.

There was a large crash and splinters of glass showered around her like an explosion of tiny hailstones. Her reaction was automatic: she ducked even lower, pulling the coat even further over her head. There were a few shrieks around her. Sebastian's head shot around. 'Sienna?'

His gaze met hers. He was worried. And he wasn't worried about himself. And for the tiniest second he wasn't thinking about Gabriel. He was thinking about her.

She didn't have time. She didn't have time to think about what that might mean. The cramped position was uncomfortable and baby wasn't hesitating to let her know it.

'His colour. How's his colour, Sebastian?'

Sebastian quickly looked back to Gabriel. 'It's better,' he said. 'He's still pale but the blueness is gone.'

Sienna breathed a sigh of relief. 'Put the monitor on his finger and tell me the reading.'

The sirens were getting much louder now; the ambulances must be almost there.

Sienna started grabbing some more of the supplies. Swabs, tape, some saline. She unwound the oxygen mask from the canister.

'Ninety-one. His reading is ninety-one. Is that good?' She could see the anxiety on his face. His steady resolve was starting to fade a little.

If she were in a hospital she'd say no. But since they were cramped under a car with a little boy bleeding and on his side she remained optimistic. Sebastian had done a good job. She was surprised at how good he'd been. He had no background in medicine. No training. But he hadn't hesitated to assist. And the weird thing was he'd been so in tune with her. He'd done everything she'd instructed. He'd been calm and competent, and somehow she knew inside that she wouldn't have expected Sebastian to act in any other way.

She took a deep sniff. No smell of petrol. No reason to deny Gabriel oxygen. She switched on the canister and unwound the tubing, pushing the mask towards Sebastian. 'Try and hold this in front of his mouth and nose. Let's see if we can get that level up a little.'

Something green flashed to her side. The knees of a paramedic as he bumped down beside her. He lifted the edge of her coat. 'Hey, Doc, it's you.'

She jerked at the familiar voice and felt a wave of relief. Sam, an experienced paramedic she'd met on a number of occasions, gave her a worried smile. He glanced upwards. 'I'm getting you out of here. Tell me what I need to know.'

She spoke quickly. 'There's a little boy trapped under the car. He was in his buggy. He looks around three. His name is Gabriel. His mother is being cared for at the side by someone.' She almost stuck her head out from the coat to look around but Sam shook his head. She pointed under the car. 'He was blue. My friend had to move him into the recovery position and he's bleeding. His sats are ninety-one. There's oxygen under there too.'

Sam nodded solemnly. He didn't remark on the fact Gabriel had been moved. He just peered under the car. 'Who's your friend?'

She hesitated. 'Seb—Sebastian. He's just visiting.'

Sam had never been slow. 'Oh, the mystery Prince everyone's talking about. Is he a doctor?'

She pretended not to hear the first part of the conversation. 'No, he's not a doctor. He's just been doing what I told him to do.' She patted her stomach. 'I couldn't quite fit.'

Sam nodded and jerked his head. 'Right, move away and stay under that coat. Back away slowly. I'll get your friend to come out and I'll replace him.' Another siren came screaming up behind them. 'That'll be Fire and Rescue. They'll help with the car and the glass.' He gave her another look. 'Now move, pregnant lady, or I'll admit you with something or other.'

She gave a grateful smile. Sam wasn't joking. She backed away to let him do his job. She heard him give Sebastian a few instructions then, in the space of under a minute, Sebastian slid out from under the car and Sam replaced him. His colleague appeared with the Fire and Rescue crew and everything just seemed to move quickly.

Sebastian moved over to her and wrapped his arm around her shoulders. 'You okay?'

There was a tiny smudge of blood just above his eye. She felt in her pocket. No tissues. They'd used them.

She gave a nod. His jeans and jacket were muddy and dirty—as was her cream coat. Truth was, it would never recover. She shivered and pushed her arms into the damp coat. 'I'm fine.

Give me a minute and I'll find something to clean your face.'

He shook his head, just as there was a shout and another shard of glass fell from the shattered shop window. Sebastian winced. But he didn't try and pull her away. He must have known she'd refuse. Instead they waited for another fifteen minutes as the Fire and Rescue crew worked alongside the paramedics and police to help all the victims of the accident.

Now she had time to take her breath she could survey just how bad things looked. The two drivers were quickly extricated from the cars, neck collars in place, one conscious and one still unconscious.

A policewoman was standing with Gabriel's mum. The poor woman looked terrified. Once the hanging shards of glass had been safely cleared from the shop window, the fire crew surrounded the car and, on instruction, just bodily lifted it to allow Sam to slide out from underneath with Gabriel on a sliding board. The buggy was still tangled around his legs.

Sienna drew in a sharp breath as her baby kicked in sympathy. Half of her wanted to rush back over and offer to help, but she knew that

Sam and his colleague were more than qualified to do emergency care. Gabriel didn't need cardiac surgery—trauma wasn't exactly her field, and part of being a good physician was knowing when to step back.

Sebastian didn't rush her. He didn't try to hurry her away from the site of the crash. As they watched all the accident victims being loaded into the ambulances he just kept his arm wrapped firmly around her shoulders.

She was glad of it. The temperature seemed to have dropped around them and the underlying shiver hadn't left her body.

A few of her colleagues who'd also helped at the scene came over and spoke to her. One of the midwives gave a wry smile. 'Can't remember the last time I treated a seventy-year-old man.' She shook her head as she headed back towards the hospital main entrance.

Sienna turned to Sebastian. 'I think it's probably time for us to go.'

He nodded and glanced down at their clothes and smiled. 'Somehow I think dinner should wait.'

She put her hand to her mouth. 'We can't go in that gorgeous car while we're so mucky.'

As they walked towards the car he let out a laugh. 'That's the beauty of a leather interior—any dirt will wipe clean. Don't worry about it.'

Her stomach gave a growl. 'Let's pick up some take-out,' she said quickly.

Sebastian gave a little frown. She almost laughed out loud. He was a prince. The last time he'd eaten take-out he'd probably been a university student. She made a note to ask Oliver about that. For all she knew, Sebastian had arrived at university with his own chef. It was time to show him how the other half lived.

He held open the door for her again. She shot him a wicked smile. 'What will we have—Chinese? Indian? Pizza? Or fish and chips?'

He made something resembling a strangled sound and gave a sort of smile. 'You choose,' he said as he closed the door and walked around to the other side of the car.

She waited until he'd climbed in. 'Pizza it is, then. There's a place just five minutes from where I live. It does the best pizzas around here.'

She settled into the comfortable seat. Even the smell in the car sent little shivers down her spine. It was gorgeous. It was luxurious. It just felt… different from anything she'd been in before.

Sebastian started the engine. It was a smooth ride; even the engine noise was soothing.

She gestured to the sleek black car following behind them. 'Do they follow you everywhere?'

He gave a little shrug. 'It's their job. They've learned to be unobtrusive. I promise, you won't even know that they're around.'

She smiled. 'Do you have to buy them dinner too?'

He laughed and shook his head. 'Don't worry. They'll make their own arrangements.'

She gave him directions, pointing him to the pizza shop.

When they pulled up outside she went to open the door but he grabbed hold of her hand. 'No way. You stay where you are. I'll order. What would you like?'

Part of her wanted to refuse. But she'd spent so long outside in the freezing temperatures that her body was only just starting to heat up. She didn't answer straight away and he prompted again. 'What's your favourite pizza?'

'What's yours?'

Their voices almost came out in sync. 'Ham, onion and mushroom.'

Silence. Both of them stared at each other for a second and then both started laughing.

She shook her head. 'Seriously? Really?'

He nodded. 'Really.'

She held up her hand. 'Wait a minute. Deep pan or thin crust?'

He glanced outside at the thick snow that was falling around the car. 'Somehow, I think tonight has to be deep pan night.'

She gave a thoughtful nod. 'I think you could be right.'

She reached out and touched his hand, narrowing her eyes suspiciously. 'Seriously, when was the last time you ate pizza?'

He winked and climbed out of the car. 'That's for me to know and you to guess. Give me five minutes.' He slammed the door and ducked into the pizzeria.

She watched while he placed his order and talked away to the guys behind the counter. Within a few moments they were all laughing. She, in the meantime, was kind of fixated on the view from the back.

She was ignoring the grime and mud all down one side of his probably designer jeans and staring instead at the distinctive shape of his broad shoulders and muscled arms under his leather jacket. If she followed the gaze down to the jeans...

Her body gave an inadvertent shudder as baby decided to remind her of his or her presence. It felt odd having the same urge of sensations she'd felt the last time she'd been around Sebastian. It seemed like a lifetime ago now. And yet...it felt as if it had just happened yesterday.

But it hadn't been yesterday, it had been months ago.

And months ago she hadn't been this shape. Months ago, she hadn't needed to adjust her position every few minutes in an attempt to try and get comfortable. Months ago her breasts hadn't virtually taken over her body. Months ago she hadn't spent her days considering where the nearest loo was.

Months ago she'd been happy to toss her clothes across the bedroom floor and let the sun streaming through the windows drench her skin.

She sighed and settled back into the seat.

Then sat straight back up again.

Her house. She would be taking Sebastian to her house.

Now they weren't having dinner at some random neutral venue. They were both covered in mud. She'd need to invite him in, and to clean up.

Sebastian. In her home.

The place where she'd made plans. The nursery that was almost finished. The wooden crib that had arrived and was still in its flat-pack box as she was so disappointed by it.

The drawer with tiny white socks and Babygros.

Her stomach gave another leap as she saw Sebastian give the guys a wave and pick up the large pizza box. How would it feel to have Prince Sebastian Falco in her home?

It was almost as if the atmosphere in the car had changed in his absence. Sienna seemed a little tense as he handed her the pizza box. She gave him stilted directions to her house and one-word answers on the five-minute drive.

He had to admit the smell from the pizza box wasn't too bad. The last pizza he'd eaten had been prepared by a Michelin-starred chef. But somehow he knew that wasn't something he should share with Sienna right now.

Earlier, he'd felt the connection to her. It didn't matter he'd been completely out of his depth and—truth be told—a tiny bit terrified of doing something wrong under that car. But every ounce of his body had told him he had to help. There was no way he could leave an injured child under a car on his own, and, with Sienna's instructions, he'd felt confident to just do as she asked.

It didn't help that the whole time he'd been under there he'd been thinking about the perilous glass dangling directly above the car and Sienna's body.

They turned onto a tree-lined street. Each house was slightly different from the one next to it. Most were painted white, and most were bungalows. A few had sprawling extensions and others had clearly extended into the roof of their property.

Sienna pointed to the left and he pulled up outside a white bungalow with large bay windows and a bright red door. It was covered in a dusting of snow and there were little white lights strung around one of the trees in the front garden.

It wasn't a castle. It wasn't a mansion house. It wasn't even a chalet in the mountains. But he could sense her air of pride. He could instantly tell how much she loved this place.

He gave her a smile. 'It's lovely.'

She let out a deep breath as her eyes fixed on her home. 'Thank you. I love it.'

He walked around quickly, holding the door open for her and lifting the pizza box from her hands. She opened the garden gate and they walked up the path to the front door.

Warmth hit them as soon as she opened the front door. She gave him a smile. 'I have a wood-burning stove. Costs next to nothing. I stack it full in the morning and it burns all day. I'd hate to come home to a cold house.'

A cold house. There was just something about the way she said those words. Almost as if cold didn't only refer to the room temperature.

She walked through to the kitchen and took the pizza, sliding it into her bright red Aga stove. She bit her lip as she turned towards him. 'I don't really have anything you can change into. You can clean up in my bathroom if you want. There are fresh towels in there if you want to use the shower.'

He could tell she was a little uncomfortable. He had no problem taking a shower in Sienna's home—it might actually help warm up his bones a little—but he didn't want to make her feel any more uncomfortable than she already did. He tried not to stare at his surroundings. There was tinsel looped over the fridge. An advent calendar with doors open hanging on the wall, and an array of little Santa ornaments lining the window ledge. Sienna really did love Christmas.

'Do you want me to leave?'

He almost held his breath.

'No. No, I don't.' She slid her dirty coat from her shoulders. 'Look, I'm going to put this in the wash. Leave your dirty clothes at the bathroom door and I'll wash them too. There's a white bathrobe on a hook behind the door. You can wear that while we eat dinner.'

He gave a little nod and walked down the corridor depositing his jeans and T-shirt outside the bathroom door. By the time he'd showered—and scoped out the bathroom for any non-existent male accessories—the pizza was back out of the oven and she had some glasses on the table.

He almost laughed out loud. The dressing gown covered him. But not entirely. His bare legs were on display and, although he'd managed to tie the waist, it gaped a little across his broad chest. It was clear Sienna was trying to avoid looking too closely.

He sat down at the table opposite her and adjusted it as best he could. 'It's not like you haven't seen it all before,' he half teased.

Colour flushed her cheeks. She lifted up the diet soda and started pouring it into glasses. 'Yeah, but I haven't seen it sitting at my kitchen table. Things that happen in Montanari tend to stay in Montanari.'

He tried not to flinch. It was a throwaway comment. He pointed towards her stomach as she served the pizza onto plates. 'It seems that what we did didn't want to stay in Montanari. It wanted to get right out there.'

He was doing his best to lead up to something. He'd had four phone calls today from the royal family's publicist. The British media knew he was here. The whitewash about twinning the two hospitals had quickly came unstuck. Any investigative journalist worth their salt wouldn't take too long to find out why he was really here. He expected to be headline news tomorrow.

She set down his plate with a clatter and before she could snatch her hand away he covered it with his own. 'Sienna, are you okay?'

She shot him an angry glance and walked around to the other side of the table and sat down, staring at him, then the pizza, then him again.

He folded his arms. 'Okay, hit me with it. It's time we were honest with each other.'

She pressed her lips together for a few seconds, then blurted out, 'Why are you here, Sebastian? What is it—exactly—that you want from me?'

He sighed. 'I'm here because of you, Sienna. Even if I hadn't heard about the baby I would never have gone through with the marriage to Theresa. I'm not my parents. I can't live that life. No matter how much they want me to.' He stared at the woman across the table from him.

She had little lines around her eyes. Her hands were spotless but there was one tiny mud splash on her cheek. Her pale skin was beautiful. Her light brown eyes looked tired. Her blonde hair had half escaped from the ponytail band at the nape of her neck. Her cheeks were a little fuller than when they'd been together last; her whole body had blossomed and it kind of suited her.

In short, he'd never seen anyone look so beautiful.

'Baby or not, I would always have come back for you, Sienna,' he said quietly. 'I thought marriage was about a union between countries. I thought I could tolerate a marriage to a friend. But as soon as it was announced I felt as if the walls were closing in around me. It wasn't enough. I'm not built that way. I just hadn't realised it. A marriage to Theresa would have made her miserable, and me miserable. It could never have lasted.'

There was silence in the room. The only sounds from the ticking clock on the wall and the rumble from the washing machine in the next-door utility room.

She licked her lips. Those luscious pink lips that he ached to taste again. 'I don't believe you,' she whispered. 'You want the heir to your kingdom. You don't want me. I was just the stranger to have sex with.'

There was hurt—hurt written all over her face. A face he wanted to cradle in his hands.

He took his time to choose his words. 'It was sex. It was great sex. With a woman who managed to crawl under my skin and stay there. A woman who has haunted my dreams—day and night—ever since. The baby is a bonus, Sienna. A wonderful, beautiful bonus that I'm still getting my head around and I get a little more excited about every day.'

Part of what he'd said was true. She had got under his skin. He'd thought about her every single day. He'd just not ever considered making her his Queen.

But this baby? This baby was too important. In a way, it would be easier if it weren't Sienna that was having his baby. Theresa had been easy to put in a little box in his head. She was a friend. She would only ever be a friend.

But Sienna? She was spreading out of any little box like a new and interesting virus. One that had started reproducing the first second that he'd met her. He couldn't squash her into some box in his head.

Because he *felt* something for her.

He just wasn't entirely sure what that was—or what it could be.

Fear flashed across her eyes and her hands went protectively to her stomach. 'This is my baby, Sebastian. Mine. I get to choose. I get to say what happens. You haven't been here. You can't just show up for the grand finale and expect to be the ringmaster at the circus. This is my life. Mine.'

He couldn't help it. Emotions were building inside him. He hated that she felt this way. 'But I want it be ours. I want it to be *our* lives. You're writing me off before we've even started. You have to give me a chance. Look at tonight. Look at how we fitted together. Do you think I could have done that with anyone else?' He shook his head. 'Not for a second, Sienna. Only with you.'

He stopped. He had to force himself. He picked up a slice of pizza even though his appetite had left him. 'Let's try and relax a little. It's been a big night. We need some down time.'

He could see a dozen things flitting behind those caramel eyes of hers.

'Stuff it,' she said as she stood up quickly. She marched to the fridge and brought out a white box that came from a bakery. She lifted out the biggest chocolate éclair he'd ever seen and put it on a plate and shrugged. 'Figure you might as well see how I deal with stress. It might give you a hint for the future.'

He sat quietly, trying not to smile as she devoured the chocolate éclair with a fork and sipped her diet soda. The atmosphere slowly settled.

From the table he could see outside into her snow-covered back garden, framed by the now black sky. It was bigger than he'd expected with an unusual style of seat and a large tree. Next to the seat was a little bush with a string of glowing multicoloured lights that twinkled every now and then.

He smiled. 'You really do like Christmas, don't you?'

She raised her eyebrows. 'Wait until you see the front room.' She sighed as she stared at her back garden. 'I've been here less than a year. I have visions of what my back garden should look like. Our local garden centre has a whole host of light-up reindeers and a family of penguins.' She pointed at the large tree. 'And I wanted lights for that tree too, and a light-up Santa to go underneath. But if I'd bought everything I wanted to, I would have bankrupted myself. So, I've decided to just buy one new thing every year. That way, I can build myself up to what I really imagine it should look like in my head.'

He watched her as she spoke and couldn't help but smile. The more she spoke, the more of a drifting-off expression appeared in her eyes, it was almost as if she were actually picturing what she wanted her garden to look like.

'Why do you like Christmas so much?'

She gave a throwaway shrug. 'I just like what it means.' She paused and bit her lip. 'It was the one time of year my parents didn't fight—probably because my Aunt Margaret came to stay.'

She smiled. 'It was almost as if she brought the Christmas spirit with her. She had so much energy. So much joy. When I was little she made every Christmas special. She was obsessed by it. And I guess I caught a little of her bug.'

It was nice seeing her like this. He stood up and lifted his glass of diet soda. 'Okay, hit me with it. Show me the front room.'

She laughed and shook her head as she stood up. This time she didn't avert her eyes from the dressing gown that barely covered him. She waved her hand. 'Give me a second.' Then she walked along the corridor and bent down, flicking a few switches just inside the door. She smiled and stood back against the wall. 'I wanted to give you the full effect.'

He stopped walking. She was talking about her front room. He knew she was talking about her front room. But he was already getting the full effect. The full Sienna McDonald effect. Every time she spoke with that lilting Scottish accent it sent blood rushing around his body. Every time their gazes connected he felt a little buzz.

She looked excited. It was obvious she was proud of whatever he was about to see.

The main lights in her room weren't on. They weren't needed, because every part of the room seemed to twinkle with something or other.

He stepped inside. The tree took pride of place at the large bay window. The red berry lights twinkled alongside the red decorations. In the corner of the room were three lit-up white and red parcels of differing sizes. A backlit wooden nativity scene was set out on a wooden cabinet. The pale cream wall above her sofa was adorned with purple and white twinkling stars.

In the other corner of the room were a variety of Christmas village ornaments. All had little lights. He smiled as he noticed the school room, the bakery, the shop and Santa's Christmas workshop.

The one thing he noticed most about this place was the warmth. Nothing like his Christmases in the palace in Montanari. Oh, the decorations had been beautiful. But anonymous people had arrived and assembled them every year. There was no real connection to the family. Everything was impersonal. Most of the time he was told not to touch. Sienna's home had a depth that he hadn't experienced before.

He turned to face her. 'It's like a Christmas grotto in here. How long did this take you?'

She shrugged. 'Not long. Well…maybe a few days.'

He stepped a little closer. Close enough to feel her swollen stomach against his. The rest of the room was dark. He reached up and touched the smudge on her cheek. 'You didn't get a chance to clean up, did you? I wonder how little Gabriel is doing.'

She froze as soon as he touched her cheek. Maybe it was too familiar a gesture? Too forward of him. The tip of his finger tingled from where he'd come into contact with her skin. He couldn't help but touch her again. This time brushing her cheek as he tucked a wayward strand of hair behind her ear.

Her eyes looked darker in here. Or maybe it was just the fact her pupils had dilated so much, they were currently only rimmed with a tiny edge of brown.

'I'll phone the hospital later.' Her voice was husky, almost a whisper. If she objected to his closeness she hadn't said.

He took in a deep breath. A deep breath of her. There it was. The raspberry scent of her sham-

poo, mixed with the light aroma of her subtle perfume and just the smell of her. For Sebastian it
was intoxicating. Mesmerising. And sent back a
rush of memories.

His fingers hesitated around her ear. He didn't
want to pull them away. He didn't want to be out
of contact with her.

This felt like something he'd never experienced
before.

Something worth waiting for.

She bit her bottom lip again and he couldn't
stop himself. He pulled her closer and met her
lips with his. Taste. He could taste her. The
sweetness of the éclair. Now, he truly was having a rush of memories.

The memory of her kiss would be imprinted
on his brain for ever. Her lips slowly parted and
his fingers tangled through her hair, capturing
the back of her head to keep her there for ever.

Her hands wound around his neck as she tilted
her head even further to his. Somehow the fact
that her swollen belly was next to his was even
better than he could have imagined. Their child
was in there. Their child was growing inside her.
In a few weeks' time he'd be a father. And no

matter what his parents might think, he couldn't wish for a better mother for his child.

His hand brushed down the side of her breast and settled on her waist.

He felt her tense. Slow their kiss. He let their lips part and she pressed her forehead against his. Her breathing was rapid.

He stayed like that for a second, letting them both catch their breath.

'Sebastian,' she breathed heavily.

'Yes?'

She lifted her heavy eyelids to meet his gaze. 'You have to give me a minute. Give me a few seconds. I need to go and change.'

He stepped back. 'Of course. No problem.'

He'd no idea what that meant. Change into what?

She disappeared into the corridor and he sank down into her comfortable red sofa for a few minutes, his heart thudding against his chest.

Maybe she wanted him to leave. Maybe she wanted him to stay.

He'd always been confident around women. He'd always felt in charge of a relationship. But things were different with Sienna.

Everything was at stake here.

Sebastian didn't do panic. But right now, if he said the wrong thing, he could mess up everything. And what was the right thing to say to a pregnant woman who'd already told you she wanted the fairy tale?

He looked around the room. The Christmas grotto. Sienna's own personal fairy tale. No castle. No prince. Just this. He tried to shift on the sofa but it was almost impossible. It was one of those sink-in-and-lose-yourself-for-ever kind of sofas.

Sienna had a good life here. She had a house that she loved. Loyal friends and the job of her dreams. The truth was, she didn't really need him. If Sebastian wanted to have a place in her life he was going to have to fight for it.

And he had to be sure what he was fighting for.

He'd meant it when he told her he'd always have come back for her. At first, it had just been words. He just hadn't said the next part—he just wasn't entirely sure what he was coming back *for*.

Someone to have a relationship with? An affair?

Or something else entirely?

It hadn't even been clear in his head until that moment. But as he'd watched her face he'd had a second of pure clarity—sitting across the table was exactly what he wanted. Tonight had given him a new perspective. If he hadn't been there he didn't doubt that Sienna would have put herself in harm's way to try and help that child. It was part of what he admired so much about her.

This might not be the way he had planned it. But Sebastian was always up for a challenge.

Sienna walked back into the room. She glanced at the gaping dressing gown and looked away. 'Your jeans are washed. I've put them in the dryer. They won't be long.'

He nodded. 'Thanks. Now, come and sit down. It's been a big day. Sit for a while.'

He could see her hesitation. See her weighing up what to do next. She'd washed her face, pulled her hair into some kind of knot and changed into what looked like pyjamas.

She walked over and sat down next to him, curling one leg up underneath her. He wrapped his arm back around her shoulder.

Sienna wanted things to be by her rules. He wanted to keep her happy.

'Tell me what you've organised for the baby. What would you like me to do?'

She looked at him in surprise. 'Well, I've pretty

much organised everything. I've turned one room into a nursery. I just need to give it a lick of paint and some of the furniture has arrived. But I haven't built it yet.'

'Let me do that.'

She blinked. 'Which one?'

'Both. All of them. Do you know what colour you want for the nursery? I could start tomorrow.'

Had he ever painted anything in his life? What did he actually know about room decoration? It didn't matter. If that was what she needed for the baby, then he would find someone to do it. Money wasn't exactly an object for Sebastian. If he paid enough, he could get it done tomorrow.

She drew back a little. It was all he could do not to focus on those lips again. He was trying his best to keep her at arm's length. Even though it was the last thing he wanted to do. If he wanted a chance with Sienna and with his baby, he would have to play by her rules.

'Well, okay,' she said after what seemed like for ever. She pushed herself up from the sofa. 'Come and I'll show you the nursery.'

He tried to follow her and fumbled around on the impossible sofa. 'How on earth did you do that? This thing just swallows you up like one of those sand traps.'

She started laughing. 'It does, doesn't it? It was one of the first things I bought when I got my own flat. I love the colour and, even though it needs replacing, I've never found another sofa quite the colour that I love. So I keep it. The removal men just about killed themselves carrying it down three flights of stairs when I moved from my flat to here.'

He gave himself an almighty push and almost landed on top of her. 'Oh, sorry.' His hand fell automatically to her waist again. It hadn't been deliberate. Not at all. But not a single part of his body wanted to move.

This was his problem. His brain was screaming a thousand things at him. He was getting too attached. He was beginning to feel something for Sienna. Something other than the blood rushing through his body. The rational part of his brain told him she didn't really want him, she didn't want to be part of the monarchy in Montanari. She was probably the most unsuitable woman to be his wife.

But little question marks kept jumping into his thoughts. Was she really so unsuitable? She was brilliant. She had a career. She was a good person. Yes, she was probably a little unconventional. She certainly didn't hesitate to speak her mind. But, after spending his life around people who didn't say what they meant, it was actually kind of refreshing. Add that to the fact that even a glimpse of her sent his senses into overload…

She pulled back a little from him so he dropped a kiss on her forehead and stepped away. 'Blame the sofa.' He smiled.

She showed him across the hall to the nursery. So far he'd seen the bathroom, the main room, the kitchen and the utility. Two other doors in the corridor seemed to glow at him. One of them must be her bedroom.

He waved his hand casually. 'This is a nice house. What's down there?'

She looked over her shoulder. 'Just my bedroom and the third room, which is a dining room/bedroom. I hadn't quite decided what I wanted to do with it yet. There's another sitting room at the back, but the house layout is a little awkward. I think the people that built the house added it on at the last minute. It ended up being off the utility room.'

Sebastian gave a nod as she flicked the switch on the room she'd designated the nursery.

It was a good-sized room. There was a pin board on the wall covered in messages and cut-out pictures. Some were of prams, some of other nurseries, some of furniture and a few of tree-houses and garden play sets.

He smiled as he looked at them all. She pointed to one of the pictures. 'That one. That's what I decided on.'

It was lovely. A pale yellow nursery, with a border with ducks and teddy bears and with pale wooden furniture.

She nodded towards the flat boxes leaning against one wall. 'It only arrived yesterday.' There was a kind of sad twang in her voice.

He walked towards it. 'What's wrong?'

She sighed. 'Nothing. It's just not quite what I'd hoped for. I'm sure it will look fine once it's all built. But there was no point in building it until I'd painted the room and put the border up.'

One of the ends of the flat-pack furniture box was open and he peered inside, reaching in with his hand to touch the contents. He got it. He got it straight away. The furniture on the picture on her pin board looked like solid oak with delicate carving and professional workmanship. Furniture bought from a store would never compare. He knew exactly what he could say right now, but he had to be careful of her feelings. She'd worked hard to make preparations for their child.

'Do you know what shade of yellow you want?'

She pointed to the corner of the room. There were around ten different little squares of varying shades of yellow. 'Yeah, I picked the one three from the end. I've bought the paint, I was planning on starting tomorrow.'

She walked over to a plastic bag. 'I have the border here, along with the matching light shade and bedding.'

He took a deep breath as he walked a little closer. 'I really want to help. I really want to be involved. Will you let me paint the room for you tomorrow? And hang the border? Once that's done I can build the furniture, and if you don't like it we can see if there's something more suitable.'

This was the point where she could step away. This was the point where he could end up flung out of the house. But she stayed silent. He could see her thinking things through. The reserve that she'd built around herself seemed to be slipping a little, revealing the Sienna that he'd connected with in Montanari.

His finger wanted to speed dial someone right now. There had to be someone around here that could help make good on his promises.

She nodded slowly then met his gaze with a gentle smile. 'Do you know what? That might actually be good...thanks.' She narrowed her gaze and wagged her finger at him. 'But you're not allowed to bring in someone else to do it. You have to do it yourself. I don't want anyone I don't know in my house.'

There was a tiny wave of unease. She could read him like a book. 'Of course. Of course, I'll do it myself. It will be my pleasure.' He looked around the room. It would be nice with the pale yellow colour on the walls.

He'd tell her things on a need-to-know basis.

He walked back to the pin board and pointed at the prams. 'Have you ordered one yet?'

The two on the board were both brightly coloured with modern designs. Nothing like the coach-built pram he'd been pictured in as a child. He gave a little smile, thinking about his room as a small child with its dark furniture and navy blue drapes.

She stepped up next to him. 'What are you smiling at?'

He gave a sigh. 'I know nothing about prams. But they both look kind of funky. I'm sure I won't have a clue how to put them together.'

Her gaze changed. It was thoughtful. Almost as if she'd finally realised that he planned on being around. Planned on being involved.

'You can buy a plain black one if you want,' she said softly. There was something sad in her voice.

His hand reached down and he intertwined his fingers with hers. 'I'll be proud to push whatever red or purple pram you choose. Why don't you let me buy you both? That's if you haven't ordered one yet.'

She paused. She hadn't pulled her hand away. He started tracing little circles in the palm of her hand with his thumb. 'Sienna, I'm here because I want to be here. I want to be here for you, and for our baby. But…' he turned to face her straight on '…this might all get a little pressured. I have to tell my parents that they're going to be grandparents.'

Her eyes widened. 'They don't know?'

'Not yet. I wanted to speak to you first. To give you a little time.' He reached and tangled his fingers through her hair. 'Once I tell them, the world will know. You won't just be Sienna McDonald, cardiothoracic neonatal surgeon any more. You'll be Sienna McDonald, mother of Prince Sebastian Falco's child. I want to protect you from that. You'll be bombarded with phone calls and emails. Everyone will want a little piece of you.' He shook his head. 'I don't want that.' He gave her a sorry smile. 'There's not enough of you to go round.'

For a moment she looked terrified. Surely, she must have expected this at some point. Surely she must have realised that the press would be interested in their baby?

Maybe his concerns about her had been right.

Her response was a little shaky. 'I don't want people interfering in my life. I'm a surgeon. I do a good job. I've made plans on how to raise this baby.'

Something twisted inside him. He wanted to say everything he shouldn't. He might only have known about this baby for a couple of weeks but every sleepless night had been full of plans for this child too.

Somehow he had to find a way to cement their plans together. There would need to be compromise on each side. How on earth would Sienna cope with his mother?

His mother's idea of compromise would be to sweep this baby from under Sienna's nose, transport the baby to the palace in Montanari and bring up the child with the same ideals she'd had for Sebastian.

For about ten seconds that had been his plan too. Had he really thought Sienna would be happy to marry him and leave her job and friends behind?

He could see himself having to spend the rest of his life having to prevent Sienna and his mother from being in the same room together.

It didn't even bear thinking about. There would be time enough for all that later. He had to start slowly.

He looked around the room. Then he glanced at Sienna's stomach. He let the wave of emotions that he'd tried to temper flood through him. That was his baby in there. *His.*

He didn't want to be a part-time parent. He wanted to see this child every day. He wanted to be involved in every decision.

And the truth was, he wanted to be around Sienna too.

He touched her cheek. 'I want to be part of those plans, Sienna. That's all I'm asking.'

She stared at him for the longest time. Her gaze unwavering.

'Let me do something to try and help. Once I've spoken to my parents, can I get one of the publicists from the palace to contact you? To try and take the pressure off any queries you might get from reporters?'

She gave the briefest of nods. At least it was something. It was a start. He hadn't even mentioned the fact that he would actually have to hire security to protect her.

'You can come tomorrow. You'll need to be up early before I go to work.'

He smiled. 'No problem. I like to be up early.' He pointed to the pin board again. 'What about the prams?'

The edges of her lips turned upwards and she gave a little shake of her head. 'You've no idea how hard this is for me.'

'What?' He couldn't keep the mock horror from his voice as he put one hand to his chest. 'You mean letting someone else help? Letting someone else be involved?'

She nodded. She waved at the photos on the

board. 'I'm running out of time. I need to order the pram that I want this weekend if it's going to be here on time.' She pulled a face. 'Trouble is, I still can't choose. And the lie-down pram, buggy and car seat all go together. At this rate, if I don't choose soon, I won't even have a way to get my baby home from hospital, let alone out of the house.'

He nodded. She hadn't taken him up on the idea of getting both. 'How about we go this weekend and look again?'

She gave him the strangest look. 'Have you any idea what these places are like? The guys in the giant nursery stores always look like they've been dragged in there kicking and screaming and can't wait to get back out.'

He raised his eyebrows. 'Well, I will be different. I can't wait to spend hours of my life helping you choose between a red and a purple pram set.' He gave a hopeful smile. 'Is there coffee in these places?'

She nodded. 'Oh, yes. But you need to drink decaf in support of me. But there's also cake. So it might not be too bad.'

Finally, he was getting somewhere. Finally he felt as if he was starting to make inroads with

Sienna. They'd made a connection today that felt like it had back in Montanari.

And this wasn't just about the baby—even though that was all they'd really talked about. This was about them too.

This would always be about them.

She walked back to the door of the nursery. 'Okay, thanks. Tomorrow it is. Now let me get your clothes. The dryer will be finished by now.'

His heart sank a little. It was time for him to go. It didn't matter how much he actually wanted to stay.

He followed Sienna down the hall as she pulled his clothes from the dryer. The jeans were still warm as he stepped into them and fastened them. He put the dressing gown on top of the dryer and turned to face her.

Her tongue was running along her top lip. She was watching him. Her eyes fixated on his bare chest. He took a step towards her.

'Sienna?'

He could act. He could pull her towards him and kiss her exactly the way he wanted to. But he'd already done that tonight. This time it was important for her to take the lead.

She put one hand flat on his chest and took

a deep breath as she looked down at the floor. There was a tremble in her voice. 'You need to give me some time, Seb. It would be so easy just to fall into things again. To take up where we left off. But there's so much more at stake now.'

His heart gave a little jump. Seb. She'd just called him Seb again.

She lifted her head and met his gaze. 'I didn't expect to see you again. I didn't expect you to come.'

He placed his hand over hers. 'And now?'

'You asked me to give you a chance. I want to. I do. But I need to be sure about why we're both here. I've had more time to get used to the thought of our baby than you have. And the thought of being under the gaze of the whole world is something I hadn't even contemplated.'

He gave her hand a squeeze. Now he couldn't help himself. He stepped forward and put his arms around her.

'Let me help. Let me get you some advice. We could release a press statement together if you wanted.'

She pushed back and shook her head. 'Release a press statement? Those are words I never thought I'd hear. Just give me a bit of time, a bit of space.

One step at a time, Seb. If you want me to give you a chance, that's the way it's got to be.'

He was disappointed. He couldn't help it. He was rushing things. But being around Sienna and not *being* with her was more difficult than he could ever have imagined.

Now he felt a sense of panic. What about the press intrusion into Sienna's life? How would she cope? He was used to it. He'd been photographed since the day he was born. But, for Sienna, life was entirely different.

She loved her job. She'd trained long and hard to be a specialist surgeon. Would she be able to continue with the job she loved if she were his wife?

At first his only thought had been about duty. His duty to the mother of his child, and to his country. His proposal of marriage had only been about those things.

Now? Things were changing. Changing in a way he hadn't even contemplated. He gave a half-smile. Was this how Oliver felt around Ella?

He pulled his T-shirt over his head and reached for his leather jacket. She handed him a damp towel. 'Try and take some of the mud off it with this.'

She was so matter-of-fact. So practical. Ten seconds ago she'd been wearing her heart on her sleeve. He wiped the jacket as best he could and slid it on.

'My shoes are next to the door.' He paused; he really didn't want to leave.

She nodded. 'Okay, then. Be here early, around seven-thirty. I'll leave you a key to lock up when you're done.'

She followed him to the door and shivered as the icy blast hit as soon as he opened it. 'Stay inside,' he said quickly. 'Keep warm. I'll see you tomorrow.'

'Seb?'

He'd already gone down the first two steps and turned at the sound of her voice. 'Yeah?'

She closed her eyes for a second. 'Thank you,' she said softly, with one hand on her stomach.

He leaned forward and kissed her cheek. 'Any time. Any time at all.' Then he headed down the path back to his car.

CHAPTER FIVE

SHE DIDN'T SLEEP a single wink—just tossed and turned all night.

Eventually, she got up and phoned to check on Gabriel. It was a relief to find out he was stable and had regained consciousness.

Seb arrived early with hot pancakes for breakfast and a hire car for her to use. He was in a good mood and only teased her a little when she gave him a list of instructions, including where he was allowed to wear his shoes.

In a lot of ways he was easy to be around. It was easy to forget he was a prince. It was easy to forget he had a whole host of other responsibilities. Ones that would ultimately keep him away from her and their baby.

The first time she knew something was off was when she arrived at work. There was a TV van in the car park and a reporter was shooting a story opposite the main entrance to the hospital.

As soon as she turned into the staff car park

one of the porters gave her a nod of his head. He walked quickly to her car. 'You might want to keep your head down and go in the side door.'

She picked up her bag. 'Why? What's happening?'

'You haven't seen it?'

Her phone started ringing. She glanced at the number. Seb. She'd only just left him. Why was he ringing her already? She silenced it as Frank held out his mobile towards her.

There was a photo. A photo of her house. A photo of her and Sebastian in her doorway looking intimate.

The headline wasn't much better.

Montanari's Baby Secret

She put her hand up to her mouth. 'No. No way. Who took that photo? That was last night. Someone was outside my house?' She didn't care about her ratty hair, or the fact she was wearing pyjamas in the photo. It looked as if she'd just fallen out of bed to show Sebastian to the door—that implied a whole lot of other things. All she cared about was the fact someone had been hanging about outside her house, waiting to take a picture. Why hadn't Seb's security people seen them?

Frank glanced over at the crowd in the car park. 'What's with the different car—did you know they'd be here? Trying to throw them off the scent?' He was smiling. It was almost as if he were enjoying the fracas.

'No. My car wouldn't start last night. Sebastian gave me a lift home. This is a hire car. My car's still in the other car park.'

Frank was still watching. 'Pull your hood up and duck in the side door. I'll walk next to you.'

She glanced around the car park. It seemed to be getting busier by the second. She pulled up her hood on her cream coat and walked alongside Frank with her head down. It only took five minutes to reach her office, close the door and turn on the computer. Her phone buzzed again. Seb.

As the computer started to kick into life she sank into her chair and put the phone to her ear. 'I've seen it. Reporters are all over the hospital. I've got a job to do. I don't need this.'

'I'll deal with it. I'll speak to Oliver and see what we can do. I'll phone you later once we have a press release ready.'

She put down the phone and watched as one headline after another appeared on screen. They had her name, her age, her qualifications. There was a report about the work she'd done in Montanari. There was speculation about how exactly she and Sebastian had met.

There was even more speculation about the timing. His sudden engagement and his wedding announcement, then his even quicker plans to cancel.

There was a camera shot of the King and Queen of Montanari from earlier on this morning. Sebastian's mother looked tight-lipped and quietly furious. He hadn't mentioned them at all. She could only imagine the kind of phone call that had been.

Oliver knocked on the door. 'Sienna? Can we talk?'

She sighed and rolled her eyes. 'Are the board complaining about the *femme fatale* on their staff?'

He snorted. 'Who cares? I'm worried about you. I've called Security. They'll keep an eye out for any reporters.'

'Thank you, Oliver.'

He paused for a second, hovering around the door as only a man who was struggling to find the words could.

She rolled her eyes again. 'What is it, Oliver?'

He pulled a face. 'I've no idea what happened between you before.' Then he shook his head and smiled. 'Well, actually the evidence is there. I've known him since we were at university. He was a few years younger than me but decided to join the same rowing club. We've been friends ever since. I just wanted you to know—I've never seen him like this.'

She frowned. 'Never seen him like what?'

Oliver hesitated again. 'Never seen him act like he's in love before,' he said as he retreated out of the door.

Her head started to swim. After a few seconds she actually put it down between her knees.

Last night had been overwhelming. Having Sebastian in her home, in a state of undress and then in the middle of their baby's nursery, had felt surreal.

She just hadn't pictured it happening in her head. It had seemed so far out of reach that she hadn't allowed her head room for it.

Now, it was a reality.

Now, the man that had haunted her dreams for months was finally only a fingertip away.

But how much was he actually offering?

When he'd told her he would always have come

back for her, she'd really, really wanted to believe him. But words were easy. Everyone knew that.

And the fact was he'd left her warm bed and put an engagement ring on another woman's finger.

It didn't matter what the facts or circumstances were. It had still happened.

It had still hurt.

She would love to believe that one snowy day, out of the blue, Sebastian would have turned up on a white stallion to sweep her away from all this and declare his undying love.

But the word love had never been mentioned.

Maybe she was unrealistic. Maybe she was a fool to chase the fairy tale. But after being brought up by parents who clearly didn't love each other she could never do that to her child. Would it be even worse if she loved Sebastian and he never quite loved her? How would their son or daughter feel about being brought up in an uneven relationship blighted by unrequited love?

It was too hard to even imagine.

So, what exactly had Oliver meant? He'd never seen Sebastian in love before?

Her stomach gave a little swirl. When she'd looked into those forest-green eyes last night all she'd been able to think about was how much this guy could hurt her. How much of her heart he'd already stolen despite the walls she'd tried to put up around it.

Self-protect mode seemed easiest.

He was being kind. He was being considerate. But could it really be love and not duty?

Her head wouldn't even let her go there.

There was a knock at her door and Juliet Turner, the neonatal specialist surgeon, walked in with contraband in her hands.

'Sienna? Are you okay?'

Sienna pulled her head up from between her knees and smiled. 'Yeah. Sorry, I'm fine.'

Juliet frowned. 'It seems like I'm just in time. I thought the road to your favourite coffee shop might be lined with reporters this morning, so decided to take the hit for you. Don't worry—it's caffeine-and-sugar-free.'

She set down the coffee and a mystery package in a paper bag. 'Anything I can do for you?'

Sienna shook her head and waved at the contraband. 'You've already done it. Have I told you lately that I love you?' Juliet laughed as Sienna continued, 'How are the quads?'

Juliet smiled. 'Things are looking good. They seem to get a little stronger every day.'

Juliet's pager beeped. She glanced at it and her smile broadened. 'Charlie. Better go. Wedding plans are in the air.'

She practically danced out of the door as Sienna took a deep breath. It seemed that everyone else in this hospital had managed to find love just in time for Christmas. Max and Annabelle, Oliver and Ella and now Juliet and Charlie.

There was no way she could be that lucky too.

No way at all. The Christmas fairy dust had all been used up around here.

Her phone beeped. She opened the message. There was a photo attached that made her blink twice.

'Yuck,' she said out loud. It was from Sebastian. And it was apparently the colour she'd chosen for the baby's nursery. What she'd thought was pale yellow had actually morphed into something more neon-like. She smiled at the message.

Is this what you had in mind?

She glanced at her watch. Just over an hour and he'd already painted one wall. Too bad he'd need to paint it again.

She replied quickly.

Not quite.

Then she dabbed again.

Not at all!

Sienna jerked as her pager sounded. The caffeine-free skinny latte with sugar-free caramel toppled and some of the hot liquid spilled down her pale pink trousers.

She jumped up. 'Great.' She looked around her office. Of course. There was nothing to mop it from her trousers with—and by the time she found something the brand-new trousers would be stained for life.

She glared at the coffee Juliet had bought for her. 'That'll teach me,' she murmured.

The pager sounded again and she shook her head as she stared at the number. Labour ward. Something must be wrong.

She left the coffee and the tiny cake decorated with holly Juliet had bought to go with it lying on the table. Her appetite had abated already.

She walked quickly down the corridor to the labour ward. She could have phoned, but they usually only paged if they actually needed her.

Kirsty, one of the younger labour-ward midwives, was looking a bit frantic. 'You looking for me?' Sienna asked. This striding quickly was getting a bit more difficult.

'I need you to look at a baby. Labour went perfectly—no concerns. But since delivery the baby has been kind of flat. I called the Paeds and they told me to page you.'

Kirsty hadn't paused for breath, her words getting quicker and quicker. Sienna reached over and put her hand on her arm.

'Kirsty, tell me what I need to know.'

Her eyes widened with momentary panic, then her brain kicked into gear and she nodded. 'Caleb Reed, thirty-six plus three weeks, five pounds eleven ounces. Born two hours. He's pale, irritable and his breathing is quite raspy.'

Sienna walked to the nearest sink and washed her hands. She glanced down at her trousers. If she had a little more time she could put on some scrubs. But best not to keep the paediatrician waiting. 'Which room?'

'Number seven.'

Kirsty walked to the room and stood anxiously at the doorway while Sienna dried her hands.

Sienna gave a nod and walked inside. Lewis

Connell, one of her paediatric colleagues, told her everything she needed to know with one glance.

She gave a wide smile to the two anxious parents and held out her hand towards the father, who was perched at the side of the bed. 'Hi, there. I'm Sienna McDonald.' She left her title out of the introduction. There was time enough for that later. The man warily shook her hand. 'John,' he said, and she held it out in turn to the mother. 'Dr Connell has asked me to come and take a look at your son. Congratulations. What have you called him?'

It didn't matter that she already knew. She was trying to get a feeling about the parents and how prepared they might be for what could come next.

The mother seemed a little calmer. 'Caleb. We've called him Caleb. And I'm Lucy.' She glanced at Sienna's stomach. 'When is your baby due?'

Sienna gave a little nod. 'Pleased to meet you, Lucy and John.' She patted her stomach. 'Not until the end of January. But if I follow your example I could have him or her any day.'

The mum gave an anxious laugh. 'My waters broke when I went to collect the Christmas turkey. Can you believe that?' She looked over to her baby with affection. 'I guess he couldn't wait for his first Christmas.'

Sienna nodded. 'I guess not. Do you mind if I examine Caleb?'

'No.' It came out as a little squeak.

Sienna smiled and walked to the sink and washed her hands again. Lewis had little Caleb lying in a baby warmer. He nodded to the chart next to him and she took a quick glance. Apgar scores at birth and five minutes later weren't too unreasonable. She was more concerned with the presentation of the baby in front of her now.

She unwound her stethoscope from her neck and warmed the end.

'Definitely cardiac,' murmured Lewis. 'But I'll let you decide.'

She trusted him. She'd worked with him for a long time. Lewis was one of the best paediatricians she'd ever worked with. His knowledge base was huge over a wide range of specialities.

Caleb was struggling. It was obvious. His skin was pale. His breathing laboured. She could see his accessory muscles fighting to keep oxygen pumping around his little body. His little face was creased into a frown and his whole body moving in little irritated twitches. The thing that she noticed most was the unusual amount of sweat glistening on his little body. Instinct told her it was nothing to do with the baby warmer. She lifted the chart and looked at the temperature. It was slightly lower than expected. The pulse oximetry readings were a little lower than expected too.

'Has he fed at all?'

She looked up to Lewis and both parents as she rested her stethoscope on the little chest. Lucy shook her head. 'The midwife tried to get him to latch on, but he didn't want to. He just didn't seem ready. She said we'd try again once the doctor had reviewed him.'

She gave a nod. 'No problem. Give me a moment while I listen to his heart.'

She scribbled a note to Lewis who nodded and disappeared out of the room to get what she'd just asked for.

She held her breath while she listened. There. Exactly what she expected. The whoosh of the heart murmur confirming the disruption of the heart flow. She felt for the pulses around the little body—in the groin and in the legs, checking the temperature of the skin in Caleb's lower body.

Lewis backed into the room again, pulling the machine.

'What's that?' John stood up.

She walked towards them. 'It's called an echo-cardiogram. It will let me check the blood flow around and through Caleb's heart.'

'You think there's something wrong with Caleb's heart?' Lucy gasped and held her hands to her chest.

The words she chose right now were so important. She didn't want to distress the brand-new parents, but she wasn't going to tell any lies.

'I'm not sure. I think it's something we need to check out. He seems a little unsettled.'

John and Lucy shot anxious glances at each other. John moved over and put his arm around his wife.

Lewis had positioned the echocardiogram next to the baby warmer and was talking in a low voice to baby Caleb. Sienna gave the parents a little nod. 'Are you okay with me checking Caleb a little further?'

They both nodded. She could practically see the fear emanating from their pores. This was one of the worst parts of her job. In some cases, cardiac conditions were picked up during the antenatal scans, plans could be made in advance and parents prepared for what lay ahead. But in cases like these, there were no plans.

One minute parents were preparing for the exciting birth of their child—the next they were being told their brand-new tiny baby needed major surgery. She had a good idea that was what was about to happen for John and Lucy.

Lewis gave her the nod and she switched the machine on and spread some warmed gel on Caleb's chest. He was still grizzly. His colour hadn't improved and from the twitching of his arms and legs it was as if his little body knew something wasn't quite right.

While he'd been inside his mother and attached to the umbilical cord his cardiac system had had constant support. Now—outside? His little heart seemed to be struggling with the work.

'Hey, little guy.' She spoke quietly as she placed the transducer on his little chest wall and her gaze flickered between him and the screen. Her trained eyes didn't take long to see exactly as she suspected. She could see movement of the blood flow through the heart chambers and heart valves. She pressed a button to measure the direction and speed of the blood flow and then moved to the surrounding blood vessels.

There. Exactly as she expected. She took a deep breath and took her time. She had to be absolutely sure what she was seeing. The room was silent around her. But she'd dealt with this before. She had to make sure she had the whole picture before she spoke to the parents.

Finally, she gave a little nod to Lewis. 'Would you be able to contact Max and see if he is available?'

To his credit, Lewis barely blinked. He would know if she was looking for the other cardiac surgeon that she wanted to act promptly. He gave a brief nod and disappeared out of the room.

Sienna wiped Caleb's chest clean, talking to him the whole time, then lifted him from the baby warmer, wrapped him in a blanket and took him over to his parents. Once he was settled in his mother's arms she sat down on the bed next to them.

'Caleb has something called coarctation of the aorta. The aorta is the big blood vessel that goes to the heart.' She picked up Caleb's chart and drew a little picture on some paper for them. 'Caleb's aorta is narrower than it should be—like this. That means that his heart isn't getting all the blood that it needs. His heart has to work harder than it should to try and pump blood around his body. And this is something we need to fix.'

She paused, giving the parents a few minutes to take in her words.

'How…how do you fix it?' asked John.

She licked her lips. 'I need to do some surgery on him.'

Lucy let out a little whimper as she stared at her baby. Sienna put her hand on Lucy's arm.

'Right now, Caleb is getting a very good blood supply to the top half of his body. But his pulses are weaker in the bottom half of his body—to his legs and feet. If we don't do surgery to widen his aorta then his heart will be affected by working too hard and he could suffer from heart failure.'

Lucy was shaking her head. 'Why?' Her eyes were filled with tears. 'Why has this happened to our baby?'

Sienna nodded. These were natural questions for parents to ask. She chose her words carefully. 'There are lots of ideas around why some babies have problems with their hearts, but the truth is—no one really knows. It could be a family thing. It could be in your genes. The type of condition that Caleb has is called a congenital heart defect. Have you ever known anyone in either of your families to have something like this?'

They exchanged glances and both of them shook their heads. She gave a slow nod. 'Sometimes people think congenital heart defects can be caused by things in the environment, things around us. Other theories are it could be caused by things that we eat and drink or medicines a mum might take.' She gave Lucy's arm a squeeze. She had to be honest, but didn't want Lucy to blame herself for her baby's condition. It was important that they focused on Caleb right now.

'How often does this happen?' Lucy's voice had cracked already and tears had formed in her eyes.

This was always the hardest part—breaking the news to parents that something was wrong with the little person all their hopes and dreams were invested in.

She'd always found this bit hard. But not quite as hard as she was finding it today. She blinked quickly, stopped tears forming in her own eyes. It was hard not to empathise with them. In a few weeks' time she would be beside herself if something was wrong with her baby. It didn't matter how much she knew. It didn't matter what her skills were.

For the last few months she'd practically lived her life in a bubble. She'd been so focused on the plans. The plans about maternity leave, cover, nurseries, childminders, cribs, prams and car seats.

She hadn't really focused on the actual outcome.

The actual real live moment when she'd become a mother and her life would change for ever.

Sebastian had brought all that home to her.

Maybe it was having someone around who was so excited about their baby. She'd felt so alone before. So determined to make sure everything would be in place.

She hadn't let the excitement—or the terror—actually build.

But having Sebastian around had heightened every emotion she possessed in an immediate kind of way.

He talked about it so easily. Their baby being here. Their baby being loved. Their baby's future.

A horrible part of her thought that when he hadn't known it had actually been a little easier.

Because Sebastian wanted to be involved in *everything*.

And it was clear he had plans on going nowhere.

The door opened and Max came in. He didn't speak, just raised his eyebrows and walked over towards her.

She smiled gratefully. 'You asked how often this happens. It is rare. But not quite as rare as you might think. Around four out of every ten thousand babies born will have this condition. In some babies it's mild. For some people it's not picked up until they are an adult. Some children aren't picked up until their teenage years. John and Lucy, this is Max Ainsley. He's the cardiothoracic surgeon that is taking over from me while I go on maternity leave.'

Max didn't hesitate. He held out his hand, shaking both their hands but letting Sienna continue to take the lead.

'If you know about Caleb now, does that mean he's really bad?' John looked as though he might be sick.

Sienna moved her hand over to his arm. 'It means it's something that we need to fix, John. And we need to fix it now.' She scribbled something on Caleb's chart. 'I'm going to make arrangements to move Caleb up to the paediatric intensive care unit. You'll be able to go with him, but the staff will be able to monitor him better there. I'll arrange for him a have a few more tests—a chest X-ray and an ECG.'

Lucy's eyes widened. 'My dad had one of those when they thought he was having a heart attack.'

Sienna nodded. 'It gives us an accurate tracing of the heart without causing any problems for Caleb. Once we have all the test results Max and I will review them. The type of surgery we need to do is to widen the narrow part of Caleb's aorta. It's called a balloon angioplasty. We put a thin flexible tube called a catheter into the narrow area of the aorta, then we inflate a little balloon to expand the blood vessel. Sometimes we put a little piece of mesh-covered tube called a stent in place to keep the blood vessel open.' She paused for a second. 'If we think the angioplasty won't work, or it's not the right procedure for Caleb, then we sometimes have to do surgery where we remove the narrow part of the aorta and reconstruct the vessel to allow blood to flow normally through the aorta.'

She took a deep breath. 'I know all this is scary. I know all this can be terrifying. I understand, really, I do. But both Max and I have done this kind of surgery on lots of babies. It's a really specialised field and we have a lot of expertise.'

'Do some babies die?'

Lucy's question came out of the blue and Max glanced in her direction. It was clear he was happy to step in if she was finding this too difficult. And for the first time in her life, she was.

She gave a careful nod. 'There can always be complications from surgery. Caleb is a good weight. He isn't too tiny. The echocardiogram of his heart didn't show any other heart defects. Some babies with coarctation of the aorta have other heart conditions—but I don't see any further complications for Caleb.' She stood up from the bed; her back was beginning to ache.

'I have to warn you that surgery can take some time. We could be in Theatre for more than a few hours and I don't want you to panic. I'm going to bring you some information to read then we'll arrange to transfer Caleb upstairs for his tests. Both Max and I will come back and explain everything again, and answer any questions before you sign the consent form. Is there anything you want to ask me right now?'

Both John and Lucy shook their heads. They still looked stunned. Max put a gentle hand on her back. She'd done this kind of surgery on her own on more than thirty occasions but somehow, at this stage of her pregnancy, she was relieved she'd have a second pair of hands.

She gave a final smile at the doorway. 'Don't worry, we'll take good care of Caleb. I'll just go and make the arrangements.'

She ignored the stiffness in her back as she walked down the corridor. It was going to be a long day.

Sebastian was waiting at the end of the corridor. 'Hey,' she said. 'What are you doing here?'

He shrugged. 'I came to find you to see if we might actually make it to a restaurant tonight. I booked out a whole place so we might actually get some privacy. I thought we could try and make Christmas Eve special. But I just heard you're going into surgery.'

He made it all sound so normal and everything he'd said was true. But he was also worried about how she was, following the news story about them. Sienna seemed remarkably calm, however. She was focused. Her mind was on the job. And he admired her all the more for it.

She gave a little sigh. 'Christmas Eve is normally my favourite night of the year. I love the build-up. The expectation for Christmas the next day.' She squeezed her eyes shut for a second as Sebastian reached up and brushed his fingers against her cheek. She opened her eyes again and they met his. 'But this is the life of a surgeon,' she whispered. 'This is the life that I've chosen.'

She held her breath as he nodded slowly. Her heart thudding against her chest. He had to understand. He had to understand that this was her life. If he wanted to be part of it, he had to realise there were things she wouldn't give up—things she would never change.

He touched her cheek again and leaned forward, his lips brushing against her ear as he whispered back, 'I wouldn't have it any other way.'

Her heart gave a little swell as a few of the other staff walked past. She was jerked from their little private moment. She pointed to the elbow of his leather jacket. 'You touched the nursery wall, didn't you?' Then her mouth opened. 'You changed the colour, didn't you?'

He let out a laugh at the pale yellow stain on his jacket. A funny look passed over his face. 'Yip. I did. Those nursery walls have been painted with blood, sweat and even a few tears.' He grimaced.

'There might have been a bit of a problem with the border.'

'What do you mean?'

He made another face. 'Let's just say the painting I could just about handle. Border skills seem to have escaped me. I might need to buy you another.' He gave her a big smile. 'And I might have done something you won't be happy about.'

'What's that?' Her head was currently swimming with thoughts of the surgery she was about to perform. She didn't need distractions.

'I see what you mean about the furniture. I might have ordered a few alternatives.' He held up his hand quickly. 'But don't worry. If you don't like them, they can go back.'

His phone buzzed in his pocket. He pulled it out, silenced it and pushed it away again.

'Problem?'

He shook his head. 'Nothing I can't handle.'

'What is it?'

'Let's just say it's a mother-sized problem.'

Sienna's heart sank a little. 'How many calls have you had?'

He shifted from one foot to the other. 'I spoke to her this morning just as the press release went out. Since then, there's been another twenty calls.'

'And you haven't answered them?'

He shook his head firmly. 'I've already heard her opinion once. I don't need to hear it again.'

It was a horrible sensation. Like something pressing down heavily on her shoulders. 'Please don't fall out with your mother because of me.'

'Let me worry about my mother. You just worry about your surgery. Oliver said I can go into the viewing room and watch.'

'Oh.' She wasn't quite sure what to say. It was one thing inviting Sebastian into her home, but inviting him to watch her surgery was something else entirely. It seemed he was determined to be involved in both her personal and professional life. She wasn't sure quite how she felt about that.

He bent forward and kissed her on the cheek. 'Good luck. You'll be fantastic. They're lucky to have you.'

The doors swung open behind them and Max appeared in his scrubs. 'Let's go, Sienna. This could be a long one.'

She gave a quick nod and followed him to scrub. Right now she had a baby to focus on. Little Caleb deserved every second of her attention.

And he would get it.

* * *

The viewing gallery for the surgery was almost full. Sebastian had to squeeze his way between a couple of excited students.

Sienna appeared cool. She and Max had a long discussion with the staff around them to make sure everyone was on the same page. Then, she glanced up at the gallery as the anaesthetist put Caleb to sleep, and talked some of the students through the procedure they were about to perform. Even behind her mask he could see the brightness in her eyes—the love of her job shone out loud and clear. It made him wish he'd got to meet her while she'd been at the hospital in Montanari. 'Well, guys, I guess this isn't where any of us expected to be on Christmas Eve, but this is the life of a surgeon.' She pointed to the equipment next to her. 'We are lucky at Teddy's to have the best technology around. The whole time we perform this surgery cameras will record our every move. There are viewing screens in the gallery, which you'll be able to watch. You'll find that during surgery Max and I don't talk much. We like to concentrate on the intricacies of the operation—that's why we've explained things beforehand. We will, however, be available to answer any questions you have once surgery is over and we've spoken to Caleb's parents.'

There were a few approving nods around him.

Max walked to the opposite side of the operating table from Sienna. 'Ready?' he asked.

She nodded once and they began.

Sebastian had never seen anything like it in his life. He'd known exactly what her job was when he'd first met her, but he'd never actually seen her in action. He'd never realised just how tiny and intricate the procedures were that she and Max performed. The baby's vessels were tiny.

But Sienna was confident in her expertise. She and Max only exchanged a few words. They worked in perfect synchronisation. Little Caleb truly couldn't be in better hands.

Things started to swirl around in his head. Sienna had a gift. A gift she'd perfected over years of sacrifice and training. No matter how much his mother's words had echoed in his head this morning about duty and expectations for the mother of the heir apparent, he could never expect Sienna to fulfil the role that his mother had for the last thirty years.

Sienna had a skill and talent he could never ask

her to walk away from. Not if he really loved her. Not if he really wanted her to be happy.

It came over him like a tidal wave. The plans he'd spent today making. The guilt that had washed over him as the decorator he'd hired had painted the first wall that hideous colour. He'd paid the man more than promised and sent him on his way. The hours of rolling yellow paint onto the walls. The aching muscles and spoiled, crumpled border. The emergency phone calls. The special orders. All because he'd realised this was about trust. This was about him, doing something for their child. This wasn't about duty at all. This was so much more than that. So much more than he'd ever experienced before.

All because he wanted to win a place in this woman's heart.

It finally hit him. She was worth it. She was really, really worth it.

He didn't want to live a single day without this woman in his life.

And he'd be lucky if he could capture a heart like hers.

Caleb's tiny vessel was even more fragile than expected. It took absolute precision to try and widen the vessel and insert the stent to make it remain patent. Having Max next to her was an added bonus. Normally, she would have performed this procedure unassisted, but they both knew that Max was likely to do Caleb's immediate follow-up care so it made sense that they worked together.

Baby wasn't taking kindly to her being on her feet so long. Her back ached more than usual and her bladder was being well and truly kicked by some angry little feet.

'Sienna?'

Max's voice was much louder than usual. She glanced up sharply just as one of the instruments fell from her hand to the theatre floor.

She blinked. He was out of focus. A warm flush flooded her skin.

'Sienna? Catch her!' he shouted and it was the last thing she heard.

One second she was in the middle of an operation, the next second Sienna was in a crumpled heap on the floor. Sebastian was on his feet and racing down the stairs before he even had time to think. He banged on the theatre doors, which were protected by a code. A flurry of staff rushed past the inside of the doors towards the theatre she'd been operating in. A few seconds later two male scrub nurses were carrying her out of the theatre.

Sebastian banged the door again and one of the theatre nurses turned in surprise. She gave a little nod of her head, obviously realising who he was, and opened the door from the inside. 'I'm going to phone Oliver,' she said as she disappeared off to another room.

Sebastian rushed after the two male nurses. They were gently laying Sienna down on another theatre trolley. Their reactions automatic. One applied a BP cuff, the other stood next to her, talking quietly to her and trying to get a reaction.

It was all Sebastian could do not to elbow both of them out of the way. But they were better equipped to assist her than he was, and he had enough know-how to stand back and let them get on with it.

After a few seconds she started to come around. Groggy and—by the look of it—uncomfortable.

She took a few deep breaths, her hands going automatically to her stomach. One of the theatre nurses smiled at her. 'You decided to go on maternity leave, Sienna.'

She blinked and tried to sit up, but the other male nurse put his hand on her shoulder. 'Not yet. Give it another few minutes. Your BP was low. Let me get you some water to sip.'

Sienna groaned and put her hands to her head. 'Please tell me everything is okay with Caleb. Nothing else happened, did it? I can't believe I just stoated off the floor.'

'You what?'

Sebastian couldn't help it. Her accent seemed even thicker than normal.

The male nurse glanced at him with a smile. 'I think she means she fainted.' He moved out of the way to let Sebastian closer. 'And don't worry. Max is more worried about you than finishing off the surgery. I'll let him know you're okay. He just needs to close.'

Sienna turned to her side for a second, her face a peculiar shade of grey. 'I think I'm going to be sick.'

About ten arms made a grab for the sick bowls but they were all too late. Sienna tried to get up again. 'Don't anyone touch that. I'll clean it up myself.'

'No, you won't.' Oliver strode through the doors. 'Don't you dare move.'

Sebastian leaned across and touched her stomach to stop her getting up, just at the same second a little foot connected sharply with his hand.

'Oh,' he said suddenly, pulling his hand back.

'Try having it all day,' sighed Sienna. 'And all night.'

But Sebastian couldn't stop staring at his hand. That was his baby. *His* baby that had just kicked him.

Of course, he'd come over when he'd heard the news about Sienna—and her pregnancy bump was obvious. But he'd never actually touched it. Never actually felt his little baby moving beneath her skin.

Oliver walked around to the other side. 'I'll arrange for you to go upstairs and have a scan. We need to make sure that everything is fine—that there aren't any complications.'

Sienna sat up this time and took the plastic cup of water offered by one of the theatre nurses. 'Oliver, honestly, I'm fine. There's no need to fuss. I hadn't managed to eat before I got called into surgery. That, and my back is aching a little because I'm getting further on. I'm fine. Once I go and get something to eat, I'll be good as new.'

'You'll be on maternity leave. That's it. No

more patients. No more surgeries.' Sebastian almost smiled. It was clear from the tone of Oliver's voice that there would be no arguments.

Max came through the swing doors tugging his theatre cap from his head. 'How are you? Is everything okay?'

Her voice wavered a little. 'I'm so sorry, Max. Is Caleb okay? Have you finished?'

He waved his hand easily. 'Of course, he's fine. Don't worry about Caleb. I'll look after him.' He pointed to her stomach. 'You just worry about yourself and that precious cargo in there.'

She swung her legs off the side of the trolley. 'Let me go and get changed.' She glanced at Sebastian. 'Sebastian can take me home. I'll get take-out on the way.'

She had that determined lift to her chin but Oliver had obviously seen it before. 'No way. Not until I say. Scan first.'

She opened her mouth to argue but Sebastian cut her off. 'That would be great, Oliver. Thanks for organising that. It's really important to us to make sure that everything is fine with the baby. Those operating theatre floors are harsh.' He met her simmering gaze. 'We both want to be reassured that the baby has come to no harm.'

He'd chosen his words deliberately. There was no way she could refuse. It would make her look as if she didn't care—and that would never be Sienna, no matter how argumentative and feisty she was feeling.

She turned towards him and whispered under her breath. 'Don't tell me what to do. And I can do this myself. You don't need to be there. Why don't you wait outside?'

He felt himself bristle. He pasted a smile on his face and spoke so low, only she could hear. 'How many scans have I already missed, Sienna? Let me assure you, I have no intention of missing this one.'

She met his gaze for a second, as if she wanted to argue. Then seemed to take a deep breath and gave a tiny nod of her head.

One of the other nurses appeared with something else in her hand. 'From my secret chocolate supply. You're only getting special treatment because I love you and I expect you to call the baby after me—even if it's a boy.'

Sienna let out a little laugh and held her hand out for the chocolate. 'Thanks, Mary, I know you guard this stuff with your life. I appreciate it.'

Sebastian was trying his best to be calm. Now

that Sienna had woken up, the panic in the room seemed to have vanished.

A porter appeared with a wheelchair and, after another check of her blood pressure, she was wheeled down the corridor towards the scan room.

Christmas Eve. The staff in the maternity unit were buzzing. Placing bets on who would deliver the first Christmas baby. The canteen would be closed later tonight and as they walked past one of the rooms, Sebastian could see plates of food already prepared for the night-shift workers.

The scan room was dark, the sonographer waiting for them. 'Hi there, Sienna. I heard you took a tumble in Theatre. Slide up on the trolley and we'll get a quick check of baby.'

Sienna had just finished eating her chocolate bar and she moved over onto the trolley and pulled up her scrub top.

Sebastian gulped. There it was. A distinct sign of exactly how they'd spent that weekend together in Montanari. He watched the ripples on Sienna's skin. Their baby currently looked as if it were trying to fight its way out from under a blanket.

The sonographer put some gel on Sienna's

stomach and lifted her scanner. She paused. 'Do you know what you're having?'

Sienna shook her head. 'Let's avoid those bits if you can. I don't really want to know.'

For the first time in a long time Sebastian felt strangely nervous. He'd never been in a scan room before. Like everyone else in the world, he'd seen it on TV shows and news clips. But this was entirely different.

This was his baby.

No, this was their baby.

He watched as the black and white picture appeared on the screen. The first thing he noticed was the flickering. The sonographer held things steady for a second as she smiled at Sienna. 'Look at that, a nice steady heart-rate.'

Ah...that was the heart.

His eyes started to adjust to what he was seeing on the screen. The sonographer chatted easily as she swept the scanner around. 'Just going to check the position of the placenta and the umbilical cord,' she said simply.

'Why are you doing that?' He couldn't help but ask.

Sienna's eyes were fixated on the screen. 'She's

checking to make sure the cord isn't twisted or the placenta detached.'

Neither of those sounded good. 'What would happen if they were?'

This time when she met his gaze she looked nervous. 'Let's just say I wouldn't be getting home for Christmas.'

He moved closer, putting his hand on hers. He looked back at the sonographer. 'And is everything okay?'

The sonographer waited a few seconds before turning to nod reassuringly. 'Everything looks fine.' She pointed to a few things on the screen, 'Here's baby's head, face, spine, thigh bone and… *oops*…let's go back up. Here are the fingers. The placenta looks completely intact and the cord doesn't appear to have any knots in it.' She placed the scanner at the side of the machine again and picked up some tissues to wipe Sienna's stomach. 'Everything seems fine.'

As the picture disappeared from the screen he felt a little pang. He'd missed out on so much already. He didn't want to miss out on another thing. The baby kicked again and even though the room was quite dark he could practically pick out the little feet and fists behind the kicks.

Sienna let out a nervous laugh. 'I guess they're beginning to get impatient. There can't be much room left in there now.'

The sonographer packed away some of her equipment. 'Five weeks to go? That's when it starts to get really uncomfortable. Watch out for some sleepless nights.' She gave Sienna a wink. 'I'll go and let Oliver know that everything is fine while you two get ready.'

Sienna shook her head. 'Yeah, thanks for that, Dawn. More sleepless nights. Just what I need.'

'You haven't been sleeping?'

She'd swung her legs off the trolley and was about to pull her scrub top back down. She looked up at him. 'You might not remember, Sebastian, but I like to sleep on my stomach—' she stared down '—and the munchkin is making it a bit difficult.'

She went to pull her top down and he put his hand over hers. The baby was still kicking. *His* baby was still kicking. 'Can you wait a minute?'

He bent down, kneeling until his head was just opposite her stomach. He watched her skin closely for each tiny punch or kick. He couldn't stop the smile. 'It's totally random. You never know where the next one will be.' He looked up at her. 'What does it feel like?'

She didn't answer for a few seconds. She was watching him with a strange look in her eyes. Eventually she stretched forward and took his hand, pressing his palm to her stomach. 'Feel for yourself.'

Sienna's skin felt different than he remembered. It was stretched tight, slightly shiny. There were no visible stretch marks, nothing that made it anything but a beautiful sight.

There. A little kick beneath his hand again.

He laughed and pulled it back. The kicks kept coming so he put both hands on her stomach. He felt something else, something bigger beneath his hand, and Sienna gave a little groan. 'What was that?'

She shook her head. 'I think that might have been a somersault. It certainly felt like it.' She placed her hands next to his and leaned back a little. 'Here, I think this is one of the shoulders. The baby's head should be down by now and it looked that way in the scan. But they can still turn if they want to. It's just not that comfortable when they do.'

Her belly felt warm. And the life contained within it was just a wonder to him.

He hadn't known it would feel like this. He didn't know it *could* feel like this. And this wasn't just about the baby. He couldn't imagine ever feeling this way about Theresa if she'd carried his child. This was about Sienna too.

'Do you have a picture?'

She frowned. 'Of what?'

'Of our baby when you got the first scan. Most people get a picture, don't they?'

She looked surprised but gave a nod. 'Yes, of course I have. It's in my bag.'

'Can I see it?'

She looked around and then shook her head. 'It's in my bag. It's in the locker room. I'll get it as soon as we get the go-ahead to leave.'

He gave what looked like a resigned nod as he stood back up and lifted his hands from her stomach. It surprised her how much she wished he'd left them there. So many things were surprising her about Sebastian.

This was all about the baby. Not about her. She had to try and put her feelings and emotions in a box and keep them there. The irony of that at Christmas time almost killed her.

She could imagine the box, with all her hopes and dreams of a fairy-tale true-love romance for her, Sebastian and the baby all wrapped in glittering red paper and silver foil sitting under her beautiful Christmas tree just waiting to be opened.

Something sank deep inside her. Reality check time.

Sebastian was interested in the baby. Yes, he'd made a few gestures towards her. But no more than she would expect from a well-brought-up prince, looking after the mother-to-be of his child.

She almost laughed out loud. Exactly how many princes did she know?

She didn't even want to admit the security she felt when he was next to her. She didn't want to acknowledge the fact that, the more he hung around, the more she lost a little piece of her heart to him each day.

She couldn't admit that. She just couldn't.

She wouldn't be her mother. The woman who'd spent her whole life with a man that had never really loved her. That wasn't a life. That wasn't a relationship.

If she'd learned anything from her parents it

was that sometimes it actually was better if parents didn't stay together. The tortured strain of living in that household had become unbearable.

And although she hated her father for his actions, with her adult brain she might actually understand, just a little.

Maybe if they'd separated much earlier, she might actually have enjoyed a different kind of relationship with her parents. One where they both had the life they wanted, and she fitted around it. But would that have been any fairer to a child than the life she'd had?

Sebastian pulled his phone from his pocket. 'What do you want to eat?'

She pulled her scrub top down quickly. 'Chinese. Hong-Kong-style chicken with noodles.'

He nodded towards the door. 'Give me a minute. I'll make the call and we'll pick it up on the way home.'

The room had felt claustrophobic for a few minutes there. Once he'd felt the kick from his baby, once he'd seen his baby's heartbeat on the screen, it had all become so real.

What had started from the first second he'd seen Sienna McDonald pregnant with his child, continued with her independence and snarkiness, been embodied by her vulnerability and the kiss they'd shared and culminated in feeling his baby kick after she'd collapsed, had just all built to the tornado of seeing that flickering heartbeat and touching the stomach of the woman who currently held all his dreams.

His head just couldn't sort out where he was. Oliver had hinted at signs of love. Did his friend even know what he was talking about? The guy was running around in a pink-tinged cloud.

The conversation with his mother this morning would have poured *Titanic*-icy waters over even the most embraced by love, soul and spirit.

Duty. The word sent prickles down his spine.

He hated it. But he actually agreed. It was his duty to marry Sienna and make this child the rightful heir to the kingdom of Montanari.

He'd been brought up to believe that duty was more important than anything. It was hard to shake that off.

But the feelings he was having deep inside about this baby and Sienna? Duty didn't even come near them. These feelings were entirely different.

They penetrated his heart, his soul, his very essence.

They felt more essential than breathing.

He closed his eyes as the call connected and he placed the order in the calmest voice possible. A few people strolled past him in the corridor. As he opened his eyes again it was clear they recognised him. The TV reporters outside meant that any chance of privacy he and Sienna had was gone for now.

Something else flashed into his head—the other secret arrangements he'd made today. He just had no idea if they'd actually been pulled off. He made a quick call—sighing with relief when it ended.

Sienna appeared at the doorway with a smiling Oliver. Sebastian blinked. He hadn't even noticed him appearing. 'Take her home, feed her and don't let her come back until she's ready to deliver this baby,' he said. 'Let's go for the due date—twenty-eighth of January will be fine.'

Sienna looked a little more relaxed. 'Let me get changed. I'll just be a few minutes,' she said as she disappeared into the locker room a few doors down the corridor.

Sebastian looked at Oliver. He trusted his friend. He trusted his expertise. 'Everything okay?'

Oliver nodded. 'Everything is fine. She's had a good pregnancy. Her blood pressure is fine. But the truth is, she's thirty-five weeks. She could deliver now, she could deliver two weeks after her due date. We never know these things.' He paused. 'Are you going to be around?'

He didn't hesitate. 'Count on it.'

Oliver held out his hand towards him. 'Good. I'll see you soon.'

Sebastian shook his friend's hand. 'Can you tell Sienna I'll get the car and wait for her at the side door? It might be easier than having to face the paparazzi when we cross the car park.'

Five minutes later he was waiting right at the door in his DB5. He'd always loved this car but it wasn't exactly inconspicuous. They might be at the side of the hospital right now, but as soon as he tried to pull out of the car park, they would be spotted.

Sienna came out of the door a few minutes later, her hood over her head. She climbed into the car and closed the door. 'Oh, well,' she sighed. 'That's two cars I've abandoned in the car park now. The broken-down one and the hire car from this morning.'

Sebastian shrugged. 'Leave me to deal with it. Don't worry. Let's just get you home.'

He wanted some privacy. He wanted a chance to get her away from all this and talk about the things they should be talking about.

He stopped at the Chinese restaurant—would his stomach ever recover from this take-away food?—and collected their meal, before turning ten minutes later into Sienna's street.

She let out a gasp.

If he'd known she was going to be unwell, he probably wouldn't have put all the plans in place that he had this morning. But it was too late now.

It was all done.

Her eyes widened as the car drew closer to her house. Everything was just as he'd asked for. A large Norway spruce had been transported to her garden and covered with multicoloured twinkling lights.

Icicle lights had been hung from the eaves of her house and stars around her two large bay windows.

She put her hand to her mouth as they pulled up directly outside. She still hadn't said a word but the expression on her face said it all. 'Wait until you see the back.' He smiled.

As they walked in the entrance hall he kept one hand around her waist, leading her straight past the nursery and down to the back door. He unlocked it and held it open.

It couldn't have been more perfect.

It didn't exactly look like a Santa's Grotto—more like a little Christmas paradise. He'd added lights to the rest of the trees and bushes. A heater next to her carved wooden seat.

The light-up reindeers and penguins from the nearby garden centre had been transported to her back garden. And to make it even more perfect the whole garden was dusted with snow, which was falling in large, thick flakes.

He kept his arm around her. 'Is it what you imagined?'

Her eyes were bright as she turned towards him. 'Oh, it's even better than I imagined. I thought it would be twenty years before it looked like this.' Her smile lit up her whole face.

He let out the breath he'd been holding, waiting to see what her reaction would be. He'd wanted to do something to make her happy. She'd already told him she loved Christmas and this was the first time they would be together at Christmas.

He was praying it wouldn't be the last.

Showering her with expensive gifts would have been easy. But he already knew that would make little impact on Sienna.

He had to know what was important to her. And this was part of the little bit of herself that she'd revealed to him.

He only hoped the rest would go down so well.

He steered her back inside. 'Let's get this Chinese food before it gets too cold. And I've something else to show you.'

The words were casual but obviously sparked a memory in her brain. 'Oh, the nursery. You've painted it, haven't you? Let me see what it looks like.'

She walked quickly back inside the house, striding along the corridor enthusiastically. She flicked the switch at the doorway and stepped inside.

Now, he really did hold his breath again. Had he overstepped the mark?

She must have already had a vision in her head for how she wanted the nursery to look—he only hoped he'd captured that invisible picture.

She made a little noise—a sort of strangled sound. Was that good? Or bad?

Then she walked straight over to the new, specially carved oak cot. Ducks and bunnies were carved on both the outside ends of the cot and along the bottom bar. She ran her hand along the grain of the wood.

He heard her intake of breath. He'd taken the step of making up the cot with the bed linen she'd already bought. But along with the pale yellow walls, and the curtains that had almost been the death of him, he thought the new furniture fitted well.

She opened the new matching wardrobe and chest of drawers.

He'd replaced all the furniture she'd bought with hand-carved pale oak furniture. It was all exactly the same style, just a different quality with a price tag that most people couldn't afford. That, plus the on-the-day delivery, would have made the average man wince. But Sebastian didn't care. He wanted the best for Sienna. The best for their baby.

She let out a little laugh at the crumpled border in the corner of the room. Darn it. He'd forgotten to throw it away.

He couldn't help himself. 'What do you think? Do you like it?'

She stood for a few minutes, her eyes taking in the contents of the room. He'd even added something extra, buying her a special cream nursing chair with a little table and lamp, and placed it in the corner of the room.

She walked back over to him, shaking her head slowly until she was just under his nose. Her eyes were glazed with tears when she looked up and his stomach constricted.

'I don't like it,' she said slowly, before opening her hands out and turning around. 'I love it! It's perfect. It just looks exactly as I'd imagined.'

'It is?'

'Yes!' She flung her arms around his neck. 'I can't believe you've done this all in one day. How did you manage?' Her hands were still around his neck but she pulled back a little. 'Did you have help?' She looked a little suspicious.

'The nursery was all me. The furniture came assembled. As for the outside decorations—I left very specific instructions.'

She raised her eyebrows. 'You can actually do some DIY?'

He laughed. 'Remember, I went to university

with Oliver. The man that can barely wire a plug. So, yes, I can use a screwdriver and a paint roller.'

She was staring up at him with those light brown eyes. There was definite sparkle there.

'You did good,' she said simply.

'I did better than good,' he whispered. 'I found you.'

Her eyes widened and her lips parted a little. 'But you didn't mean to.' She glanced downwards. 'You didn't mean for this to happen.'

He shook his head. 'Neither did you. But this was always meant to happen, Sienna. I believe it. I was meant to meet you. You were meant to meet me. *We* were meant to be. This baby was meant to be. The more I see you every day, the more I can't imagine spending a single day without you.'

'But how can that be, Seb? How can that happen? I live here. You're part of a royal family in Montanari. You're the Prince, and one day you'll be the King. Somehow, I don't think I fit the job description.'

He shook his head. 'You don't get it, do you? It's up to me to think about the job description. And for me it's obvious. There's only one person I want by my side. Montanari needs to bring itself into the twenty-first century. A queen and royal mother that's a neonatal cardiothoracic surgeon? An independent, educated woman who is dedicated to her job? How can that be a bad thing? Why on earth would I ask you to give that up? I couldn't be more proud of the job that you do. I couldn't be more proud of the fact you came to Montanari to train our surgeons. I watched you in action today, Sienna. I don't think I've ever seen anything I admire more. You couldn't be more perfect if you tried.'

'I couldn't?' She looked stunned—as if it were the last thing she'd expected him to say. She looked as if she was about to say something else but he cut her off. He dropped a kiss on her perfect lips. Truth was, he'd thought about nothing else all day. She tasted sweet and as he kissed her and his fingers tangled through her blonde hair the fruity aroma from her shampoo swept around them. His hands went from her hair, to her shoulders and down her back.

He could feel their baby between them. It was stopping him getting as close as he'd like to. He intertwined his fingers with hers. 'Come here,' he whispered and pulled her through to the main lounge, sitting down on the swallow-you-up sofa and drawing her towards him.

She hesitated for the slightest second before moving forward and sitting astride him on the sofa. She looked at him for the longest time then finally lifted one hand and brushed her knuckles gently against the emerging shadow on his jaw-line. 'I don't know what to make of you, Seb,' she said in a throaty voice. 'I don't know what to make of any of this.'

He ran a finger down the bare skin on her arm. 'Tell me what you want.'

She shook her head. He saw the little shiver go up her spine as he ran his finger down her arm again. It was the gentlest of touches. The lightest of touches. They'd been intimate before. They'd been passionate before.

But not like this.

His hands settled on her stomach, feeling the baby lying under her skin. It seemed to be settled in one position. 'Do you think our baby is sleep-ing?' He smiled.

She arched her back, her stomach and breasts getting even closer. 'I hope so,' she murmured. 'But doubtless as soon as I go to bed they'll wake back up again. I think our baby is going to be a night owl and I have to warn you—' she leaned forward and whispered in his ear '—us Scots girls can get very crabbit when we have no sleep.'

He caught a strand of her hair and twisted it around one finger. 'Don't sell yourself short, Sienna. I seem to remember a couple of occasions when you managed quite well without sleep.' He released the strand of hair and let his hands brush against her full breasts then settle on her waist.

She closed her eyes and let out a little moan. Her hands pressed against his chest, her fingers coming into contact with the tiny hairs at the nape of his neck. He caught his breath. This was becoming more than he could have imagined. His body started to react.

Sienna smiled down at him. 'You like this? When I'm tired? Have an aching back? And, even though I haven't checked yet, probably puffy feet?'

'I think you're perfect just the way you are,' he said simply. He put his hands on her stomach again. 'Pregnant. Not pregnant.' He lifted his hands higher. 'Big boobs. Small boobs. Swollen feet. Not swollen feet.'

'I'm not a queen-in-waiting, Seb.' She shook her head slowly. 'I've never wanted to be.'

'You want the fairy tale. I can give you that.'

She closed her eyes for a second. 'You can give me the palace, the lifestyle, the people.' She pressed her hand against her heart. 'But what's in here? You need someone who wants to live that life. I don't think that can ever be me.'

He put his hands on her thighs. 'But our baby will be the heir. That's written in the stars, Sienna. You can't wipe that away. I want our child to grow up loving the country that they will eventually rule. I want them to respect and appreciate the people that live there. I want the people of Montanari to love my family.'

He sucked in a deep breath. 'We should get married, Sienna. Think about it. We could make this work between us, and we could make this work as a family. Don't dismiss me out of hand like you did before. Take your time. Think about how we both want to bring our child up. Think about what's important to you.'

What was important to her? Right now her head was so muddled she couldn't think straight. Her breath had stalled somewhere in her throat. He had passion in his eyes when he spoke about Montanari. Just like the flicker she'd seen in his eyes a few moments earlier when they'd been locked in an embrace.

But when she'd pressed her hand against her heart, he just hadn't picked up what she'd meant. She wanted to know what was in *there*. In that heart that was beating in his chest.

Because no matter how hard she'd tried to fight it, she'd developed feelings for Sebastian. Feelings that she just couldn't be sure were reciprocated.

He'd focused on part of her fairy tale—but not the most important part. The part that meant she and her Prince loved each other with their whole hearts. The part that she just couldn't live without.

Sebastian lit up her heart in a way she didn't want to admit. She couldn't put herself out there to find her love dismissed. The stakes were too high.

He was talking about Montanari. Making it sound as if that should be the place they have a future together. Lots of women might love that. A prince. A castle. A new baby.

But if he really knew her, he would know that a vital component was missing.

Something gripped her. Something tight,

knocking her breath temporarily from her lungs. 'Oh.' She held out one hand towards Sebastian and gripped the other around her stomach.

'Sienna? Is everything okay?' He shifted position, moving her from his knees and onto the sofa.

She was stunned. 'I don't know. I've never felt anything like that before.'

His eyes widened. 'You don't think that…' His voice tailed off. His face paled.

She was still catching her breath, wondering where the sharp pain had come from and hoping against hope it was something else entirely.

She stood up and started pacing. Sebastian was right by her side. This couldn't be happening. It was too early. She was only thirty-five weeks.

'You had that fall today—do you think it could be anything to do with that?'

Sweat started to break out on her skin. She looked from side to side. 'I'm not ready. I'm not ready for this. I should have another five weeks to think about this—to make plans.'

Tears prickled in her eyes. 'It's Christmas Eve. I was planning on watching some TV and wrapping some final presents.'

Sebastian glanced at the enormous pile under the tree. 'You have more?'

He slid his arm around her waist and she batted him on the chest. 'Stop it.'

He turned her around to face him.

One tear slid down her cheek. He brushed it away with his finger. 'Should I phone an ambulance? Oliver told me to phone if I was worried. Should I do that now?' He was babbling. The Prince was babbling.

It felt like an out-of-body experience. He'd always seemed so in control. Or at least he wanted the world to think that.

'Will our baby be okay? Will you be okay?'

Another tear slipped down her cheek. 'I'm thirty-five weeks today. They might give me some steroids to bring the baby's lungs on, and baby might be a little slow to feed. But there's nothing else we should worry about.' She slid her hands across her stomach. 'But, if I think I'm not ready, then I know for sure that you're *definitely* not ready.' Her heart started thudding in her chest. She'd operated on tiny babies. She'd been doing it for years and years. But she'd never actually *had* a baby before. And the truth was, she was scared.

Scared of what could lie ahead.

She broke out of his hold and started pacing again. 'I had everything planned. I knew what was happening. Then—' she turned to face him and held up her hand '—you come along with your kingdom and your press team, and your let's-twin-our-hospitals, and you've just confused me, stressed me—'

'You're saying all this is my fault?' She could see the pain and confusion written all over his face.

Then—*whoomph*. This time it was stronger. This time it made her bend double. *'Oohh.'*

'Sienna?'

Her hands went back to her stomach; she slid them under her loose top. This time there was no mistake. She could feel the tightening under the palms of her hands.

Sebastian strode towards her just as something else happened.

Something wet and warm. All over her living-room oak floor.

She closed her eyes.

'Is that what I think it is?'

She nodded and looked down at the darkening wet stain on her trousers. Thank goodness they were pale—otherwise she'd be panicking she couldn't tell the colour of the liquid. This liquid was clear.

'Start the car, Sebastian.'

'You don't want an ambulance?' There was an edge of desperation to his voice.

'On Christmas Eve? In the Cotswolds? We can get there much quicker on our own.'

In less than five minutes she'd changed and thrown some things into a bag; another contraction slowed her down. The front door was wide open, showing the snow-covered garden outside. Sebastian was standing with his jacket on, pacing at the front door. The car was running.

'Let's go. I'll lock up.'

She let him guide her out to the waiting car.

She groaned as he climbed in next to her. 'This wasn't what I imagined for Christmas Eve.'

He cleared his throat and shot her a nervous glance. 'Actually, I can't think of anything more perfect.'

'What?'

'We're having a baby.'

She took a deep breath and tried to clear her head. Focus. All she could focus on right now was the fact they were about to meet their child.

She had to have some head space. She had to be in a good place.

'Truth is, I'm a tiny bit terrified,' she whispered, staring out at the snow-topped houses and glistening trees. Next time she came back here she'd have a baby with her.

His hand closed over hers. 'Then, let's be terrified together.'

CHAPTER SIX

'IT'S A GIRL!'

'It is?' Sienna and Sebastian spoke in unison.

Ella, the midwife in the labour suite and Oliver's new fiancée, smiled up at them as she lifted the baby up onto Sienna's chest. 'It certainly is. Congratulations, Mum and Dad, meet your beautiful new daughter.'

Sebastian couldn't speak. He was in awe. First with Sienna and her superwoman skills at pushing their baby out, and now with the first sight of his daughter.

She looked furious with her introduction to the world. Ella gave a little wipe of her face and body as she lay on her mother's chest and she let out an angry squeal. Ella laughed. 'Yip, she's here. Have you two thought of a name yet?'

A name.

His brain was a complete blank.

He still couldn't process a thought. He could have missed this. He could have missed this once-in-a-lifetime magical moment. That couldn't even compute in his brain right now.

His daughter had a few fine blonde hairs on her head the same shade as her mother. He had no idea about her eyes as her face was still screwed up.

'She just looks so…so…big,' he said in wonder.

Sienna let out an exhausted laugh. 'Imagine if I'd reached forty weeks.' She looked in awe too as she ran her hand over her daughter's bare back. 'She's not big. She's not big at all. Ella will weigh her in a few minutes. But let's just wait.'

Sebastian shook his head as Ella busied herself around them. 'I have no idea about a name.'

He wanted to laugh out loud. For years in Montanari, the royal family were only allowed to pick from a specific list of approved names. His mother still thought that should be the case.

Sienna turned to him. 'I think we should cause a scandal. Let's call our daughter something wild—like Zebedee, or Thunder.'

Now he did laugh out loud. 'I think my mother would have a fit. It's almost worth it just to see the expression on her face.'

Sienna was still stroking their daughter's skin. 'Actually, I do have a name in mind.'

'You do?'

She nodded. 'I'd like to call my daughter after my aunt. She was fabulous with me when I was growing up and looked after me a lot when my mother and father were busy.'

She didn't say the other words that were circulating in her brain. *Or when my mother and father couldn't be bothered.*

It was an unfair thought and she knew that. But she was emotional and hormonal right now. She'd just done the single most important thing she would ever do in this life.

Her parents had never mistreated her. They just hadn't been that interested. Her aunt had been different. She'd always been good to her.

'What's your aunt called?'

Their daughter started to stir, squirming around her chest and making angry noises. 'Margaret,' she said quietly. 'My aunt was called Margaret.'

It was the last thing he'd really expected. A traditional name from an untraditional woman.

'Really?'

She looked up and met his gaze. Her hair was falling out of the clip she'd brought with her for the labour. Her pyjama top was open at the front to allow their baby on her skin.

He'd never seen anything more beautiful.

He'd never seen anything he could love more.

He blinked.

It was like a flash in the sky above him. He'd been trying to persuade Sienna to give him a chance for all the wrong reasons. He'd always liked her. The attraction had never waned.

But duty still ran through his veins. In his head he'd been trading one duty marriage for another. But Sienna had bucked against that.

She demanded more. She *deserved* more.

And it was crystal clear to him why.

He didn't want to have to persuade her to be with him. It was important to him that she wanted to be with him, as much as he wanted to be with her.

And she'd need to be prepared for the roller coaster that was his mother.

Sienna was more than a match for his mother— of that he had no doubt. But sparks could fly for a while in the palace.

His father—he was pretty sure he would love her as soon as she started talking in her Scottish accent and telling it exactly as it was.

Ella gave him a nudge. 'Do you want to hold

your daughter? Sienna's work isn't quite finished yet.'

Sebastian gave an anxious nod as Ella first took their daughter from Sienna, weighed her, put a little nappy on her and supplied a pink blanket to wrap their daughter in. Two minutes later she gestured for him to sit in a comfortable seat she pulled out from the wall. 'Once she's delivered the placenta, we'll do another few checks. Oliver will arrive any minute. And I'll arrange for some food for you both. After all that hard work you'll both be exhausted. We have plenty to spare in the labour ward.'

He hardly heard a word. He was too focused on the squirming little bundle that had just been placed in his arms. The smile seemed to have permanently etched itself onto his face. It would be there for ever.

Her face was beautiful. He stroked her little cheek. The wrinkles on her forehead started to relax and her eyes blinked open a few times. He'd been told that all babies' eyes started as blue. His daughter's were dark blue; they could change to either green like his, or brown like her mother's. The blonde hair on her head was downy, it already had a fluff-like appearance and he could see the tiny little pulse throbbing at the soft centre in the top of her head.

He couldn't have imagined anything more wonderful. Less than twenty minutes ago this tiny little person had been inside Sienna, a product of their weekend of passion in Montanari. She might not have been planned but, without a doubt, it was the best thing that had ever happened to him.

They were the best thing that had ever happened to him.

Sebastian shook his head. 'Sienna did all the hard work. I was just lucky enough to be here.' He lifted one hand that had been thoroughly crushed for the last few hours. 'I might need a plaster cast, but I can take it.'

Ella smiled and went back to work.

By morning Sienna was back in a fresh bed with a few hours' sleep, showered and eating tea and toast. Margaret had finally opened her eyes and was watching him very suspiciously—as if she were still trying to work out what had happened.

Oliver came into the room to check Sienna over. 'Trust you not to hold on. You never did have any patience. I'm going to relish the fact that your daughter has obviously inherited your genes. Good luck with that, Sebastian,' he joked. He put his arm around Ella. 'Seriously, guys, congratulations. I'm delighted for you.'

He gave a nod towards the door. 'Word travels fast around here. There are a few more people who want to say hello.'

Ella looked to Sienna. 'How do you feel about that?'

Sienna glanced over at Sebastian, cradling their baby girl. 'Tell them to come in now. I want to try and give our daughter another feed. I think she'll get cranky quite soon.'

Ella gave a nod and Annabelle and Max, and Charlie and Juliet crowded into the room. Sebastian held his precious daughter while they all fawned over her, kissing Sienna and congratulating them both.

Charlie nodded at the clock on the wall. 'If you'd just held off for another few hours you could have had our first Christmas baby.'

Christmas. Of course. He'd almost forgotten this was Christmas Day now.

Sienna looked shocked for a second then threw back her head and laughed. 'Darn it! I completely forgot about that!' She looked suspicious for a second. 'Did any of you have a bet on me for the Christmas baby?'

Juliet shook her head. 'Not one of us. No one expected you to deliver this early.' She leaned over Sebastian's shoulder. 'But your girl looks a good weight for thirty-five weeks. What was she?'

'Five pounds, thirteen ounces,' answered Sebastian. Margaret's weight would be imprinted on his brain for ever.

Just as this moment would. Now he'd held his daughter, he didn't ever want to let her go.

Sienna's stomach grumbled loudly as she finished the toast. 'Sorry,' she laughed to her visitors.

She was trying to pay attention to them—she really was. But she couldn't help but be a little awed by the expression on Sebastian's face at the bottom of the bed. He was fascinated by their daughter. He could barely take his eyes off her.

She felt the same. She was sure she wouldn't sleep a wink tonight just watching the wonder of her little daughter's chest rising and falling.

'Here.' Annabelle thrust a little gift towards her. 'Something for your gorgeous girl.'

Sienna was amazed. 'Where on earth did you get a present on Christmas Day?'

Annabelle gave her a wink. 'I have friends in high places.'

Sienna felt her heart squeeze. Annabelle was the most gracious of friends. Sienna knew how hard she and Max had tried for a baby of their own; it had eventually broken down their marriage until their reconciliation a few weeks ago. And yet here they both were, celebrating with her and Sebastian over their unexpected arrival.

She opened the gift bag and pulled out the presents. A packet of pale pink vests, a tiny pink Babygro that had a pattern like a giant Christmas present wrapped with a bow, matching tiny pink socks and a pale pink knitted hat with a pompom bigger than Margaret's head. She laughed out loud.

She'd bought a few things for the baby's arrival but, with the rush, she'd forgotten to bring them from home. 'Oh, Annabelle, thank you, these are perfect. Now we have something to take our daughter home in.'

Sebastian looked up quickly, pulling the little bundle closer to his chest.

'We're going home?'

Oliver shook his head. 'No, sorry. Not tonight. The paediatrician wants to be sure that Margaret is feeding without any problems. I'm afraid you'll need to spend your daughter's first Christmas in hospital.' He glanced at Ella. 'Don't worry, the staff here are great. They'll make sure you're well looked after.'

Sienna sagged back against her pillows. 'I don't care. She's here, and she's healthy. That's all I care about. I might love Christmas. But it can wait.'

Max looked around the room. 'Let's say our goodbyes, folks, and leave the new parents with their baby.' He rolled his eyes. 'Some of us have Christmas dinners to make.' Right on cue Margaret gave out a scream that made Sebastian jump.

Everyone laughed. They quickly gave Sienna and Sebastian hugs and left the room. Sienna pushed the table across the bed away and held out her hands. 'I think she must be hungry. Let's see if she's ready for a feed.'

Ella came back a few minutes later and helped Sienna position their daughter to feed. The first feed had been a little difficult. She gave Sienna a cautious smile. 'Sometimes babies that are born a little early take a bit longer to learn how to suck.

They all get there eventually, but it can take a bit of perseverance.'

Sienna's eyes were on their daughter. 'It seems Margaret doesn't like to wait for anything. As a first-time mum I expected to have one of those twenty-hour labours.'

Ella shrugged. 'You might have done, if you'd reached forty weeks. You might be quite tall, but your pelvis is pretty neat.' She smiled up as Margaret latched on. 'Just remember that for baby number two.'

Almost in unison Sebastian and Sienna's heads turned to each other and their wide-eyed gazes met, followed by a burst of laughter.

Sienna waved her hand at Ella. 'Shame on you, Midwife O'Brien, mentioning another baby when the first one is barely out. You haven't even given me time yet to be exhausted!'

A warm feeling spread throughout Sebastian. His daughter's little jaw was moving furiously as she tried to feed. Sienna seemed calmer than he'd ever seen her, stroking her daughter's face and talking gently to her.

Ella looked up and met his contented gaze with a smile. 'I'll leave you folks alone for a while.

Come and find me when you want some food, Sebastian. I take it you're staying all day?'

'Can I?' He hadn't even had a chance to discuss with Sienna what happened next.

Ella nodded. 'Of course. All new dads are welcome to stay with mum and baby. This is Teddy's. We're hardly going to throw you out on Christmas Day. This is a time for families.' She winked and left the room.

Sienna lifted her head and looked at the clock. 'I can't believe we had her on Christmas Eve. It all just seems so unreal. I thought I would spend today lying on my sofa, like a beached whale, watching TV and eating chocolates.'

A special smile spread across her face. 'I thought I wouldn't see you until next Christmas,' she whispered to their daughter. 'I'd planned to buy you one of those Christmas baubles for the tree with your name, date of birth and baby's first Christmas on it. I guess you've ruined that now, missy.'

Although she loved Christmas dearly, she'd been edgy about this year. Worried about what the future would hold for her and her baby. Sebastian showing up had brought everything to the forefront.

He was sitting in a chair at the end of the bed. Ever since her first labour pain he'd been great. After that first flicker of panic he'd been as solid as a rock. He'd rubbed her back, massaged her shoulders, and given her words of constant encouragement during the few short hours she'd been in labour. All without a single word of preparation. They hadn't even got around to the discussion about whether he would attend the labour or not.

He hadn't even blinked when she'd turned the air blue on a few occasions, and chances were he'd never regain the feeling in his right hand. She hadn't had time to think about whether he should be there or not. And the look on his face when he'd first set eyes on their daughter had seared right into her soul.

She'd never seen a look of love like it. Ever.

And that burned in ways she couldn't even have imagined.

'Seb?'

'Yes?' He stood up. 'Do you need something?'

She shook her head, trying to keep her wavering emotions out of her voice. 'I wouldn't ever have kept her from you. I would have told you about her as soon as she arrived,' she said quietly. She blinked back the tears.

She saw him swallow and press his lips together briefly. They were both realising he could have missed this moment. Missed the first sight of his daughter. Was it really fair that she'd even contemplated that?

She licked her lips. 'Your mother—what has she said about all this?'

For a few seconds he didn't meet her gaze. 'She's disappointed in me. That I didn't do things in a traditional way. She thinks I treated Theresa badly. She hasn't quite grasped the fact that Theresa was marrying me out of duty—not of love.' His eyes met hers and he gave a rueful smile. 'I think it's just as well I'm an only child. She would have tried to disown me at the beginning of the week because of the scandal I've caused.'

'But what does that mean? What does that mean for you, for me and for Margaret?'

Something washed over her, a wave of complete protectiveness towards her daughter. She wasn't going to let anyone treat Margaret as if she were a scandal—as if she weren't totally loved and wanted.

Sebastian sat down on the edge of the bed next to her and wrapped his arm around her shoulders. 'It means that I'll have to phone the Queen and tell her about her new granddaughter. She thought there would be a few weeks to try and manipulate the press. I guess our daughter had other ideas.'

The thought of the press almost chilled her. 'Can we keep her to ourselves for just a few more hours?' She hated the way that her voice sounded almost pleading. But this was their daughter, their special time. She wasn't ready to share it with the world just yet.

'Of course.' He smiled. His fingers threaded through the hair at the nape of her neck. It was a movement of comfort, of reassurance.

Her hormones were on fire. Her heart felt as if it had swollen in her chest, first with the love for her daughter, and next for the rush of emotions she'd felt towards Seb in the last few hours.

Everything that had happened between them had crystallised for her. His sexy grin, twinkling eyes and smart comments. The way his gaze sometimes just meshed with hers. The tingling of her skin when he touched her.

The way that at times she just felt so connected to him.

All she felt right now was love. Maybe she was a fool to expect more than he already offered. She could live in Montanari. He had no expectations of her giving up work—she could work with the staff she'd trained in their specialist hospital.

Margaret could be brought up in a country she would ultimately one day rule. And although that completely terrified Sienna, it was a destiny that couldn't be ignored.

Did it matter if Sebastian didn't love her with his whole heart? He respected her—she knew that. And he would love their daughter.

This might be simpler if she didn't already know the truth.

She loved Sebastian. She'd probably loved him since that first weekend—she just hadn't allowed her brain to go there because of the betrayal that she'd felt. How hard would it be to live with a man, to stand by his side and know that he didn't reciprocate the love she felt for him?

Could she keep that hidden away? Would she be able to live with a neutral face in place in order to give their daughter the life she should have?

She pressed her lips together. Having just a little part of the man she loved might be enough. Having to look at those sexy smiles and twinkling eyes on a daily basis wouldn't exactly be a hardship.

And if he kept looking at her the way he did now, she could maybe hope for more. Another child might not be as far off the agenda as she'd initially thought.

She looked up at those forest-green eyes and her whole world tipped upside down. 'Your mother's name—it's Grace, isn't it?'

He nodded but looked confused.

She stared back down to her daughter's pale, smooth skin. 'I've had the name Margaret in my head for a while. But I had never even considered any middle names.' She looked up at him steadily. 'That seems a bit of a royal tradition, isn't it?'

He nodded again. She could see the calculations flying behind his eyes. 'What do you think about giving Margaret a middle name?'

The edges of his lips started to turn upwards. 'Seriously?'

She nodded, feeling surer than before. 'I chose our daughter's first name. We never even had that discussion. How do you feel about choosing a middle name?'

She'd already planted the seed. Maybe the Queen wouldn't hate her quite as much as she imagined.

He looked serious for a second. 'Our family has a tradition of more than one middle name—how do you feel about that?'

She frowned. 'You mean you're not just Sebastian?'

He laughed. 'Oh, no. I'm Sebastian Albert Louis Falco.'

She leaned back against him. 'Okay, tell me what you're thinking. Let's try some names for size.'

He took a few seconds. 'If you agree, I'd like to call our daughter Margaret Grace Sophia Falco.' He turned to face her. 'Unless, of course, you want to call her after your mother.'

Something panged inside her. But the tiny feelings of regret about her relationship with her parents had long since depleted over time. 'No. I'm happy with Margaret. I think it's safe to say that my mother will play her grandmother role from a distance.' She glanced at the clock. 'I'll let both my parents know in a while about their granddaughter. I doubt very much that either of them will visit.' She gave a sad kind of smile. 'I might get some very nice flowers, though.'

She looked down at Margaret again, who'd stopped feeding for now and seemed to have settled back to sleep. 'Who is Sophia?'

Seb smiled. 'My great-grandmother. In public, probably the most terrifying woman in the world. In private? The woman I always had the most fun with. She taught me how to cheat at every board and card game imaginable.'

Sienna couldn't help but smile. 'You mean that the Falco family actually had some rogues?'

He whispered in her ear. 'I'll show you the family archives. We had pirates, conquerors and knights. We even had a magician.' He leaned over her shoulder and touched their daughter's nose. 'Happy Christmas, Margaret, welcome to the Falco family.'

Sienna turned to face him just as his lips met hers. 'Thank you, Sienna. Thank you for the best Christmas present in the world.'

She reached up and touched the side of his face. Her head was spinning. He was looking at her in a way she couldn't quite interpret. Her heart wanted to believe that it was a look of love, a look of hope and admiration. He hadn't stopped smiling at her—and even though she knew she must look a mess, he was making her feel as if she were the most special woman on the planet.

'Thank you,' she whispered as her fingers ran across his short hair. 'We made something beautiful. We made something special. I couldn't be happier.'

'Me either,' he agreed as he pulled her closer and kissed her again.

CHAPTER SEVEN

HE'D HARDLY SLEPT. He hadn't wanted to leave the hospital last night, but both he and Sienna had been exhausted. She only ever cat-napped when he was in the room and he'd realised—even though he hadn't wanted to be apart from them—that it would be better if he let her spend the night with their daughter alone.

Not that she would have had much time. He'd left the hospital at midnight and was up again at six, pacing the floors in her house, itching to go and see her and Margaret again.

His mother's voice had been almost strangled when he'd phoned with the news. But after a few seconds of horror, she'd regained her composure and asked if Sienna and baby were healthy after the premature delivery. He'd assured her that they were.

When he'd told her the name of her new grand-daughter there had first been a sigh of relief and then a little quiver in her voice. 'I'm surprised that such a modern woman picked such a traditional name. It's a lovely gesture, Sebastian. Thank you. When will we see the baby?'

He sent his mother some pictures of Margaret and told her he'd invited both Sienna and Margaret to join him in Montanari. He hoped and prayed that they would, but placated his mother with the easy opt out about travelling so soon after delivery and making sure that Margaret's little lungs would be fit to fly.

He stood in the middle of the yellow nursery that Sienna had dreamed of for her daughter. If she agreed to join him in Montanari he would recreate this room exactly the way it was—anything to keep her happy.

Things had been good yesterday. They'd been better than good. Sienna and Margaret were his family, and that was exactly how they felt to him. He couldn't imagine spending a single day without them. He'd had a special item shipped yesterday from the royal vault at Montanari. It was still dark outside but the twinkling lights from the Christmas tree across the hall glinted off the elegant ruby and diamond engagement ring in his hand. He hadn't mentioned this to his mother yet. But with Margaret's new middle names, it was only fitting that Sienna wear the engagement ring of his great-grandmother Sophia.

The two of them would have loved each other.

He'd meant to go back to his hotel last night but Sienna had asked him to collect the baby car seat from the house so they could be discharged today. Once he'd arrived back at her house he'd decided just to stay. It had seemed easier. He should have brought some of his clothes from the hotel, because this was where they would come back to in the first instance.

He hurried outside to his car. It didn't really matter what time it was—the hospital would let him in any time. He just wanted Sienna to have had a chance to rest.

As soon as he pulled up outside the hospital alarm bells started going off in his head. Every TV station with a van was parked near the entrance. Every reporter he'd ever met was talking into a camera.

Someone spotted his car. All he could hear was shrieks followed by the trampling of feet. He got out of the car in a hurry. One of the reporters thrust a newspaper towards him. 'Prince Sebastian. Tell us about your new arrival.'

'Congratulations. What have you called your daughter?'

They surrounded him. Security. He hadn't considered security for his daughter. He stared at the news headline in front of him.

A NEW PRINCESS FOR MONTANARI!

The questions came thick and fast.

His hand reached out and grabbed the paper. He hadn't agreed to a press release. He had discussed it with his team and they'd planned an announcement for later today, once he, Sienna and baby Margaret had left Teddy's.

How on earth did the press know about Margaret already? He looked a little closer and felt his ire rise. There was a picture of his daughter. *His daughter.* Wrapped in a pink blanket, clearly lying in her hospital cot. Who on earth had taken that?

He started to push his way through the crowd of reporters. He didn't manhandle anyone but he didn't leave them in any doubt that he would reach his destination.

'Prince Sebastian, what about Sienna McDonald, the baby's mother? Are you engaged? Are you planning a royal wedding?'

Right now, he wished he could answer yes. But it seemed premature. Even though things were good between them, he hadn't asked her again yet. But the enthusiasm being shown for the birth of the new Princess was more than a little infectious. These people would hang around all day. It would be smarter just to give them a quick comment—he could find out about that photo later.

He turned around and held up his hands. 'As you know, my daughter was born a little earlier than expected on Christmas Eve. Both mother and baby are doing well and...' he paused for a second as he searched for the words '...I'm looking forward to us all being a family together very soon. Our daughter's name is Princess Margaret Grace Sophia Falco,' he finished with before turning around and walking through the main doors of the hospital.

The noise behind him reached a crescendo.

The length of his strides increased in his hurry to reach Sienna and his daughter. His hand slid into his pocket and he touched the ring again. The box had been too bulky to fit in the pocket of his jeans. But the ring was still safely there.

A few of the midwives gave him a nod as he walked towards Sienna's room. It was only Boxing Day so the decorations were still all in place and Christmas carols played in the background.

Hopefully, by the end of today, he could make things perfect for everyone.

Sienna felt cold. She had been ignoring the TV in the corner of the room and just concentrating on her baby. The midwives were great. Margaret had decided to have an episode of colic at three a.m. After half an hour, one of the midwives had told Sienna to get some sleep and she'd walk the corridor with Margaret. Sienna hadn't wanted to let her baby out of her sight, but she'd been exhausted. Two hours later she'd woken with a peaceful Margaret wrapped in her pink blanket and back in her crib.

By that time, she'd wanted to get back up. She'd had a bath to ease her aching back and legs, and fed and changed Margaret. Once Sebastian arrived she was hoping they would get the all-clear to take Margaret home.

Something caught her attention. A few words from the TV. Sebastian.

She looked up as the TV reporters camped outside the hospital all set off at a run to interview Sebastian on live TV.

She still couldn't understand how they knew about the baby. No one she worked with or trusted would speak to the press. Sebastian had said he would talk to her about a press release.

She smiled as she caught sight of him on camera. His hair was a little mussed up. He obviously hadn't taken time to fix it. His tanned skin sort of hid the tiredness she could see in his eyes. His leather jacket—still complete with yellow smudge—showed off his broad chest and his snug jeans caused her smile to broaden. Sebastian Falco. Was she really going to agree to what he'd suggested last night?

Sebastian was a seasoned pro when it came to paparazzi. He wouldn't speak to them.

But actually, he stopped.

Just like Sienna's heart.

They were all firing questions to him about Margaret. Asking him to confirm the birth and her name. Someone thrust a newspaper towards him and she saw the tic in the side of his jawline. Whatever was in that newspaper had made him angry.

Another voice cut above the rest. 'Prince Sebastian, what about Sienna McDonald, the baby's mother? Are you engaged? Are you planning a royal wedding?'

A prickle ran down her spine. How could he answer that? They hadn't even finished that discussion.

Something flickered across his face, the edges of his lips turned upwards. 'As you know, my daughter was born a little earlier than expected on Christmas Eve. Both mother and baby are doing well and...' he paused for a second as a smile spread across his face '...I'm looking forward to us all being a family together very soon. Our daughter's name is Princess Margaret Grace Sophia Falco.'

Her heart plummeted.

Oh, no. Oh, no. Did he realise how that looked?

Sure enough the reporters had a field day. A woman in a bright red coat swung around and announced straight into the camera. 'We have a royal engagement *and* a royal wedding! It seems that Dr Sienna McDonald is about to become the wife of Prince Sebastian and the future of Queen of Montanari.'

The woman's bright red lips seemed to move in synchrony with the other reporters all around her, talking into their respective cameras.

A chill swept across her skin. The woman seemed to think she'd got the scoop of the century. She held her hand up to the sign of the Royal Cheltenham hospital. 'Looks like Teddy's is going to have to find another cardiac baby surgeon.' She said the words with glee. 'Once Sienna gets to Montanari she will have no time to worry about being a doctor.'

Fury swept around her. How dared they? How dared any of them assume that she would give up her job, her house, her life?

The door swung open and Sebastian strode in with a smile. 'You're up? You're awake?' He was still carrying the newspaper that had been thrust at him in his hand. 'Great. We need to talk. We need to make decisions.'

'Haven't you already just made all those for me?' She walked right up to him. 'Who on earth do you think you are?'

He pulled back and glanced towards their sleeping bundle in the corner. 'What on earth are you talking about?'

She flung her hands up in the air. 'Oh, come on, Sebastian. You're not naïve. You've been doing this all your life. You know better than to get pulled into things.' She couldn't stop the build of fury in her chest.

He'd tricked her. He'd sweet-talked her. He'd used all that princely charm. All to get exactly what he wanted.

All to get his daughter back to Montanari.

Sebastian shook his head. 'What do you mean?' He tried to step around her—to get to Margaret.

Sienna stepped sideways—stopping his path. 'You practically just announced to the world that we were getting married.'

His tanned face blanched. 'I didn't.' It sounded sort of strangled.

She pointed to the yellow tickertape-style news headline that had now appeared along the bottom of the TV screen.

Prince Sebastian to marry Dr Sienna McDonald, mother of their daughter.

He flinched. Then something else happened. The expression on his face changed. He reached down into his pocket. 'Sienna, I didn't say we were getting married.'

'No. But with a smile on your face you just said that we were all going to be a family together soon. You practically told them we'd be moving to Montanari with you!'

He put his hands on her shoulders. 'What's wrong with you? Calm down. After last night, I thought things were good between us. I thought that maybe we were ready to take the next step.' He glanced over her shoulder. 'The right step for us—and our baby.'

She shivered. She felt as if she were in a bad movie with the villain in front of her. 'You did this,' she croaked as she looked frantically back to Margaret.

'What?' Confusion reigned over his face.

'The leak. It was you.' She pushed him away from her, forgetting for a second about Margaret as she strode forward and lifted the discarded newspaper. The picture of their baby brought tears to her eyes. 'You did this?' She couldn't actually believe it. 'To get what you wanted, you actually gave them a picture of my daughter without my permission?'

She couldn't think straight at all. She was just overwhelmed with emotions and a huge distinctive mothering urge. She'd been tricked. Manipulated. By a man she'd let steal her heart.

He'd left last night after telling her things could

work. He'd introduce her to the family. Margaret could be brought up in Montanari and they could all live together as a family. He'd let her think they'd embrace a new-style queen—even though it wasn't a title she'd wanted. She could continue with the job she loved.

Sebastian looked utterly confused and shook his head again. 'What on earth are you talking about?' He took the paper from her hand. 'You think I did this? Really? Why on earth would I do that? We talked about this last night.'

'Yes. You said you'd wait. You said we'd agree to a statement. But that obviously wasn't good enough for you. You're used to getting your own way, Sebastian. You're used to being in charge. You lied to me last night. I was wrong to trust you. You made me think you would consider my feelings in all this.' She swung her hand to the side. 'Instead, you let the world know about our baby.' Tears sprang to her eyes. 'This is my time with my baby, mine. I don't want to share her with the world. I'm not ready.' She shook her head as everything started to overwhelm her. He was just standing there, standing there looking stunned.

She kept shaking her head. Now that they'd

started, the tears just kept on coming. She was angry at herself for crying. Angry that she was standing here in her ratty pyjamas, hair in a ponytail and pale skin telling the Prince she wouldn't stand for this behaviour. She wouldn't be manipulated into more or less giving up her life and her daughter.

She'd thought there might just actually be some hope for them both. They could reconnect the way they had in Montanari. The memories that she had of the place would stay with her for ever.

There had been moments—fragments—when they'd captured that spark again. But she'd been a fool. She'd been living the fairy tale in her head. Why? Why would a prince ever love her?

Things shouldn't be like this. If she were telling him to leave, she should be doing it in some magnificent building, wearing an elegant dress, perfect make-up and her hair all coiffured. She should be looking a million dollars as she told the fairy-tale Prince he couldn't manipulate her or deceive her. That she would bring their daughter up here, rather than be promised a lifetime without love.

Because that was what it really came down to.

That was what she wanted. What she'd always wanted.

For Sebastian to love her, the way her heart told her she loved him.

The clarity in her brain made her turn on him.

'You've deceived me. You've deceived me right from the start. You've spent the last few days trying to sweet-talk me. Trying to persuade me to bring our daughter to Montanari. And now? You think if you just leak the story to the press, then give them some kind of coy smile, and tell them we're about to be a family—then that's it. A fait accompli.' She flung her hands in the air again. 'Well, no, Sebastian. No. I won't have it. I won't get trapped into a life I don't want. I won't bring Margaret up in a marriage with no love in it.'

If Sebastian had looked stunned before, now his mouth fell open. He stepped forward then froze as she continued to rant.

She pressed her hand to her heart as the tears streamed freely. 'I won't do it. I just won't. I've been there. I've already spent eighteen years in a relationship like that. A relationship where I was tolerated and not really loved.' She shook her head. 'Do you know what that feels like? Really? Do you honestly think I'd bring my daughter up in a relationship like that? It's not enough. Not nearly enough. I love you. You love her. But you don't love me. I don't want a loveless marriage. I want a husband that will love and adore me.' She looked off into the corner as she tried to catch her breath.

'A husband that will look at me as though I'm the most important person in the world. A husband that will trust me enough to always talk to me. To always be truthful with me. To support me in the job that I've trained to do since I was eighteen.' She took a step towards Sebastian. Looking into the face of the man that she'd thought would love her as much as she loved him. Being here in front of him made her stomach feel as if it were twisting inside out. It was hurting like a physical pain. That was how much she wanted this dream to come true. That was how much she wanted to be loved by him. It felt like the ultimate betrayal.

'You lied to me,' she said with a shaking voice. 'You said Montanari was ready for a new kind of queen. A queen who had a career. A queen who worked. You said that could happen. But according to the world outside, the expectation is that I give it all up. My years and years of training don't count. They don't matter. Well, they matter to me. And the environment I bring my daughter up in matters to me. I want Margaret to feel respected. To know she should work hard. To know that money doesn't grow on trees and you have to earn a living.'

She kept her voice as strong as she could. 'Your plan didn't work, Sebastian. I won't marry you. We won't be coming to Montanari.'

Sebastian felt as if he'd been pulled up in a tornado and dumped out of the funnel into a foreign land. He couldn't believe what she was saying. He couldn't believe what he was being accused of.

Worst of all were her words about being trapped inside a loveless marriage. Did she really hate him that much? She could never grow to love him even a little?

The ring felt as if it burned in his pocket. His plan had been to come in here this morning, tell her he loved her and would make this work, and propose. He'd felt almost sure she would grow to love him just as much as he loved her.

But her words of a loveless marriage were like a dagger to the heart. No matter what he promised her it seemed she couldn't ever imagine a life with him. A life with them, together as a family.

Had he really been so blind that he thought they were almost there?

Margaret gave a whimper from the crib. Twice, Sienna had stopped him walking towards her. Twice, she'd stopped him from seeing his daughter.

Sebastian felt numb.

'I'm done trying to force what isn't there. I'm done trying to be anything other than I am. You should have told me as soon as you found out you were pregnant. You should have let me know that I was going to be a father. The news blindsided me. You had months to get used to the idea. I had two weeks.'

He looked furious now.

He put his hand on his chest. 'And I wanted it, Sienna. I wanted it more than you could ever have imagined. I can't believe you're being so judgemental.' He shook his head. 'What did I say? I said I was looking forward to us all being a family together very soon. That's it. What's so wrong with that? They asked me if we were engaged and if we would get married and what did

I do? I smiled. Because a tiny little part of me actually wanted that to happen.'

He started pacing.

'Do you know why? Because I was a fool. I was a fool to think we actually could have a life together. I was a fool to think you might grant me a scrap of that affection and passion you keep so tightly locked up inside you.'

He spun around towards her again.

'Well, I'm done. I'm done trying to force this. You clearly don't know how to love someone. Or if you do, it's clear that person will never be me. I won't spend my life tiptoeing around you. Margaret is my daughter, as much as yours. I'm not going to fight with you, Sienna. I will not have my daughter witnessing her parents rowing over her. If you're incapable of talking to me about her—if you're incapable of compromise—then we can talk via lawyers. You don't get the ownership on loving Margaret. She has the right to be loved by both her parents. I want to see her. I want to spend time with her. And, even though you clearly hate me, I won't let you stop me seeing her.'

He couldn't stop the words from coming out of his mouth. This woman, Sienna, who he'd hoped would make his heart sing, had just turned his world upside down. He loved her with his whole heart. He loved his daughter with his whole heart.

This morning, he'd thought he could turn this into something wonderful. He'd had the audacity to think that he and Sienna could love each other and it could last a lifetime.

Now...?

He just didn't know.

Sienna couldn't find any more words. Sebastian turned on his heel and walked outside.

She sagged on the bed out of pure exhaustion. What had happened? The tears continued to fall and her only comfort was lifting Margaret to her chest and holding the little warm body next to hers.

Her precious daughter. *Hers.* That was what she'd said to Sebastian. It didn't matter that it had been in the heat of the moment. She'd said it deliberately to exclude him. But Margaret wouldn't be here without Seb. The facts of life were simple.

The reporter in the red coat was still talking incessantly on the TV. Now, she was talking about how delighted Queen Grace was, how angry Princess Theresa was, how the people in Montanari were waiting for a formal announcement about their new heir, and how the Prince was clearly enthralled by his new daughter and fiancée since there had been no sign of him.

All she could think about was the expression on Sebastian's face. The hurt. The shock. The surprise. The words, 'I said I was looking forward to us all being a family together.'

She screwed her eyes closed for a second. When she'd challenged him on that he'd said he'd smiled because he'd hoped they could have a life together. They would get engaged. They would get married. Something tugged at her heart. The tone of his voice. The pain in his eyes. What did that mean? Did that mean he did care about her? He might actually love her?

There was a knock at the door and one of the midwives entered. She looked uncomfortable and pale-faced. She hesitated before talking. 'Seb... The Prince. He's down at the nursery. He asked if he could see Margaret before he leaves.'

'He leaves?' She felt sick. She stared down at her daughter's face. Margaret stared back and blinked. It was as if she was trying to focus. Already her eyes looked as if they would change colour. Change colour to the same as her father's forest green.

The midwife hesitated again. 'He asked if he could see her before he returns to Montanari.'

There.

She had what she wanted.

Sebastian was going to go.

It was like being rolled over by a giant tidal wave. The isolation. The devastation.

She started to shake as she gazed at Margaret. How would she feel if the shoe were on the other foot? How would she feel if someone stood between her and her daughter?

She'd chased him away. She'd said everything she probably shouldn't have said. But she couldn't think straight right now. Her heart was already wrung out by the birth of her baby.

When Sebastian had given that smile to the reporter she had instantly judged. She'd assumed he was being smug. She'd assumed he was calculating. But what if it had been none of those things? What if he'd been entirely truthful with her?

What if...what if he'd actually meant what he'd said? He'd believed they could have a life together. But did that life include love?

She started sobbing again. She didn't want

him without love. She wanted everything. She couldn't let herself settle for anything less.

The midwife pulled tissues from a box that had miraculously appeared and handed her a few. She didn't say anything, just put a gentle hand on Sienna's shoulder.

She stared at her little daughter's face. He'd accused her of being incapable of love. She felt like just the opposite. As if she loved too much. She loved Margaret so much already. And right now? Her heart was breaking in two about Sebastian. She wasn't a woman incapable of love.

Far from it.

'What do you want me to tell him?' came the gentle voice of the midwife.

She nodded as a tear dripped from her face and onto Margaret's blanket. 'Yes. Tell him, yes. He can see Margaret.'

She handed her baby over with shaking hands.

She'd ruined everything and there was no way back.

The midwife took tentative steps down the corridor towards him, holding Margaret still wrapped in the pink blanket. His heart gave a little surge of relief. He turned back to the window of the nursery. The quads he'd heard everyone talking about looked tiny compared to Margaret. But he could see each of them kicking their legs and punching their tiny hands. Each fighting indignantly against their entry into the world. Their names were emblazoned over their plastic cribs. Graham, Lily, Rupert and Rose. He smiled. Traditional names, like Margaret. Maybe it was a new trend?

The midwife gestured with her head to the next room. 'Would you like to sit in here with your daughter?' He nodded and followed her inside, sitting in a large chair next to the window as she handed Margaret over. 'I'll wait outside,' she said quietly, then paused at the doorway. 'Sienna. She's very upset.' She sighed. 'I think you both need to take a deep breath.' She waved her hand. 'It's none of my business. I'd just hate you both to lose something that you love.' She turned and walked outside.

Sebastian stared at his daughter in his arms. His heart should be soaring. He should be celebrating. He should be rejoicing. But he'd never felt quite this sad.

This hadn't been the day he'd planned for.

This hadn't been the day he'd expected. In fact,

it was so far away from what he'd thought would happen that he could barely even believe this was how things had turned out.

It was never meant to be like this between them. Never.

Of that—he was sure.

But how on earth did they come back from this? He'd said some things he regretted. He'd said a lot of things he regretted.

He'd never been a man for emotional outbursts. He'd spent a life of control, of restraint. But Sienna brought out a side of him he'd never thought he had.

Around her, his feelings ran stronger than he thought possible.

So, it was true.

Love could cause the greatest happiness.

And love could cause the greatest misery.

Margaret grumbled in his arms. Her little head turned from side to side, probably rooting for her mother.

Could he really go home? Could he really bear to leave them and not see them for how long—a few days, a week, a month?

He shuddered. He couldn't bear that. Not at all.

Life was precious. Life was fragile. Life wasn't supposed to be like this.

What would he do if he returned to Montanari? Probably fight with his parents. Probably take his frustrations out on those around him. All because he'd messed up the most important relationship of his life.

The relationship with the woman he loved with his whole heart.

He'd tried to forget about Sienna. He'd tried to follow his parents' wishes and get engaged to someone else.

In the end, it hadn't worked. It would *never* have worked.

His heart belonged to Sienna.

And he had to believe, he *had* to believe that part of her heart belonged to him too.

Margaret was important. Margaret would always be one of his priorities. But his other priority would be the woman he wanted as his wife.

Life ahead for him was formidable. Ruling Montanari would only be possible with a strong woman by his side. A woman whom he loved and respected. A woman who could help to lead Montanari into the modern world.

Everything about Sienna had captured his

heart. Her wit. Her intelligence. Her stubbornness. Her determination. The look in her eyes when she'd first seen their daughter…

He had to win her. He had to win her back.

He'd never actually told her how he felt about her. He'd never actually put his heart on the line.

He'd been scared his feelings wouldn't be reciprocated. And that could still happen.

But he wasn't leaving her until he tried.

He stood up and walked to the door. The midwife stepped forward to take Margaret. 'No.' He shook his head. 'I'll take Margaret back to her mother.' He took a calm breath. 'I won't leave without talking to her.' He added quietly, 'I won't leave without putting up a fight for them both.'

The midwife gave a little nod of her head. 'Good luck,' she said quietly as he started down the corridor.

She'd finally managed to stop crying, wash her face and change out of the pyjamas into the clothes that Sebastian had set down in the corner for her earlier. She'd be going home soon.

Home with her daughter.

Right from when she'd started making her

plans, she'd always expected to take Margaret home on her own.

But this last week, those steadfast plans had started to wobble.

Sebastian had slowly but surely started to creep his way around the edges and somehow into the middle of them all.

The night before last, when she'd seen the beautiful job he'd made of the nursery she'd been overwhelmed. It was almost as if Sebastian had climbed into her brain and seen the picture that she had stored in there.

He'd made the dream a reality.

His face when he'd looked at their daughter had taken her breath away. And when he'd then turned and met her gaze? She'd never felt so special. She'd never felt so connected or loved.

How could she go from that point to this?

She finished rubbing some make-up onto her face. Right now, she was paler than she'd ever been. She needed something—anything—to make her look a little alive again. She couldn't find her mascara, or any blusher, and there was only one colour of lipstick in her make-up bag, so she rubbed a little furiously into her cheeks and put some on her lips.

The door swung open behind her and she stepped out of the bathroom to get Margaret from the midwife. Her boobs were already starting to ache and Margaret was probably hungry again.

But it wasn't the midwife.

It was Seb.

For a second, neither of them spoke. They just stared.

Finally Seb drew in a breath. 'You look…good.'

'That good, really?' It came out of nowhere. The kind of smart retort she'd got used to saying around him. Her eyes instantly started to fill with tears again—it was just as well she hadn't found mascara.

Margaret gave a little yelp and she held out her arms. 'Give me her. She needs to feed.'

He hesitated. And instead of handing Margaret over, he put her up on his shoulder. 'We need to talk.'

Sienna shook her head. 'We're done talking. We've said enough. We both need some space.'

He nodded. 'You're right. But just exactly how much space do you need?'

She frowned. 'What do you mean?'

He met her gaze. 'I mean, I don't want to leave.

I don't want to go back to Montanari without the two people I love.'

She froze. Part of her wanted to believe. But part of her questioned everything.

'You just want Margaret. You don't want me. Don't panic, Seb. We'll work something out. You can see her.'

He stepped closer. Margaret seemed to be sucking at his neck. It wouldn't take her long to realise there was no milk there. He touched her arm. 'You're wrong. I do want you. I've always wanted you, Sienna—even when I didn't really know it myself. I would have come back. I would have always come back for you.'

She could hear what he was saying. He'd tried to say it before. But she just couldn't let herself believe it.

'But you didn't,' she whispered. 'You only came because of Margaret.'

He closed his eyes for a second. 'Sienna, you have to believe that even if Margaret wasn't here, *I* still would be.'

It was painful when she sucked in a breath. She shook her head. 'Words are easy. I'd like to believe you but, for all I know, you might just be saying this to persuade us both to come back to

Montanari with you. This might all just be a trick to get Margaret back to your country.'

He reached over and touched her face. It was the gentlest of touches. 'Sienna, don't. Don't think like that of me. Is that really how you feel about me? I'm a liar? A manipulator?' He looked genuinely upset. His forest-green gaze held hers. 'Is that how the woman I love really feels about me?'

Her heart squeezed tightly in her chest. Her mouth was so dry she could barely speak. 'You love me?'

He stepped even closer. Margaret let out a few grumbles. His hand brushed back across Sienna's cheek and this time across her long eyelashes too.

'I love you so much I sometimes can't breathe when I think about you. I love you so much that the face I see when I close my eyes is yours. I can't let you slip through my fingers. I can't let the chance for this to become real get away because I'm emotional. You're emotional. And I'm a fool.'

She smiled. He knew how to charm a lady.

His fingers moved around her ear, tucking some stray strands of hair behind it. 'But I will, Sienna, if that's what you want. If you want me to leave—to give you space—I will. But know that I'll do it because I love you. Because you are the most important thing to me on this planet. Because I will always put what you want before what I want.'

Tears pooled in her eyes again and she took a step towards him. 'How can you do that, silly? You have a kingdom to look after. All those people. How on earth can I matter?'

He bent his head towards her. 'You matter because I say you matter. You and Margaret will always come first for me.'

This wasn't charm. This wasn't manipulation. This wasn't lies.

This was real.

'Oh, Seb,' she whispered. 'Can this really work?'

He took a deep breath. He was shaking. He was actually shaking. 'Only if you love me. Do you love me, Sienna?'

A tear dripped down her face. She reached up and touched the stubble on his jawline. Her lips trembled as she smiled. 'I do,' she whispered as she pulled his forehead towards hers.

His smile spread across his face. His eyelashes

tickled her forehead. 'I think you've said that a little too early.'

She laughed as he fumbled in his pocket. 'Give me a second.'

She held her breath as he pulled out a glittering ruby and diamond ring—bigger than she could ever have imagined. He smiled at the ring. 'This is a family heirloom. It belonged to my great-grandmother, Sophia, one of the most spirited women I've ever had the pleasure to know.' He gave her a special smile. 'She would have loved you, you know. She told me to give it to the woman that captured my heart and my soul. That's you. Will you marry me, Sienna?'

She lifted Margaret from his shoulder and tilted her lips up to his.

'A princess and a surgeon? Do you think you can cope?'

He slid his arms around her as his lips met hers. 'I can't wait to spend my life finding out.'

EPILOGUE

MONTANARI WAS COVERED in snow for the first time in twenty years. It was almost as if every weather system had aligned especially for the royal wedding.

Sienna looked at the snow-covered palace lawn, trying to hide the butterflies in her stomach. She kissed her ruby and diamond engagement ring and closed her eyes for a second.

This was it. This was when she married the man who had captured her heart, her soul and the very breath in her body. Sophia's engagement ring had been a lucky talisman for her. So much so that, when she couldn't decide on her wedding gown, late one night she'd trawled through the palace archives and found a picture of Sophia on her wedding day.

It had been perfect. A traditional gown covered in heavy lace was the last thing she would ever have contemplated. But somehow, the style reached out and grabbed her. The long-sleeve lace arms and shoulders were perfect for a winter wedding, as was the lace that covered the satin bodice and skirt. She'd taken the picture and asked the wedding designer to replicate the dress for her.

The door opened behind her and Juliet and her daughter Bea walked in. Both were wearing red gowns that matched their bouquets. Juliet gave her a smile. 'Ready, Princess?'

Sienna shook her head. 'Don't. I might just be sick all down this gown before anyone has had a chance to see it.'

Juliet walked over, her pregnancy bump clearly visible in her gown. Babies were in the air around here. She pulled at a strand of Sienna's curled hair. 'I spotted Sebastian earlier. He couldn't wipe the smile off his face. And you needn't worry about sickness. Margaret has just been sick on the Queen's outfit. I thought she was going to pass out with shock!'

Sienna threw back her head and laughed. 'Really? You mean, she'll actually have to change her outfit? Oh, I love that girl of mine. She knows exactly how to make her mother proud.'

There was a knock at the door and Oliver stuck

his head inside. 'Sebastian asked me to give you a message.'

Her heart gave a little flutter. 'What is it?'

Oliver laughed. 'Hurry up and get down the aisle. He's done waiting. It's Christmas Eve tomorrow and Margaret's birthday. You have presents to wrap!'

Sienna gave a nervous nod. 'I'm ready. Tell him, I'm ready.'

Oliver walked across the room and gave her a kiss on the cheek. 'Ella and I couldn't be happier for you.'

She smiled as he left. Ella and Oliver had got married a few months before the birth of their baby, Harry. She'd never seen him happier.

Music drifted up the stairs towards them. Juliet gave her a nod and walked around, picking up the skirts of her dress.

The wedding was being held in the royal chapel, with the reception in the palace. She'd tried to memorise all the visiting dignitaries in the hope she wouldn't make some faux pas. Queen Grace had only thawed a little in the last year. She seemed a little interested in Margaret, and when she'd made a few barbed comments about the wedding plans Sienna had happily handed over the guest list and seating plan and told her to take charge, in case she seated some feuding families next to each other.

She was learning how to manage her mother-in-law and Sebastian was entirely grateful.

They reached the entrance to the chapel and Sienna sucked in her breath. The entire chapel was lit by candles, creating a beautiful ethereal glow. Juliet rearranged her skirts then set off down the aisle with Bea. Charlie watched them the whole way, his face beaming with pride. Their wedding plans had been put on temporary hold due to Juliet's pregnancy, but Sienna couldn't wait to attend the ceremony in the Cotswolds next summer.

Oliver held out his elbow. 'Two jobs for the price of one. Do I get double the salary for this?'

She bent over and kissed his cheek. 'You get my eternal thanks for being such a good friend. I couldn't have picked anyone more perfect to give me away, or to be Sebastian's best man.' She winked as the wedding march started. 'Just remember, the wedding speech will be watched the world over. I love you, but tell any Sienna-got-drunk stories and I will lace your dinner with arsenic.'

He laughed and patted her arm. 'I'll keep that in mind. Ready?'

She licked her dry lips and nodded.

As soon as they started down the aisle, Margaret started to call to her. 'Mama, Mama.' She was being held by Annabelle while Max held their daughter, Hope. Max and Annabelle had renewed their wedding vows and, after adopting Hope, were hoping to adopt two boys who were in foster care in North Africa.

Margaret was tugging at Annabelle's hair with one hand and waving at Sienna with the other. Her cream dress was rumpled—she crawled everywhere—and her headband was almost off her head. Margaret was destined to be the biggest tomboy in the world.

Sienna stopped to kiss her little hand, then carried on the last few steps to Sebastian.

He didn't hesitate. He took her hand immediately. 'You look stunning,' he said simply.

'You don't look too bad yourself.' She smiled. His athletic frame filled the royal dress uniform well, the dark green jacket making his eyes even more intense. Her heart skipped a few beats.

They fought regularly and made up even more passionately. He'd helped prepare her for the new role she'd have in Montanari and supported her in every decision she'd made. She'd started working between both hospitals but, to Oliver's disappointment, had made some plans recently to work permanently in Montanari. Sebastian didn't know that yet.

The music started to play around them for the first hymn and he leaned over and whispered in her ear. 'I didn't think it was possible, but I love you even more each day.' His thumb traced a circle in her palm. 'Ready for two to become one?'

She smiled at him with twinkling eyes. 'Actually, it's three becomes four.'

He blinked. Then his eyes widened and his smile spread from ear to ear as Sienna started to laugh.

And that was the picture that made the front page of every newspaper around the world.

* * * * *

We hope you enjoyed the final story in the
CHRISTMAS MIRACLES IN MATERNITY
quartet

And, if you missed where it all started,
check out

THE NURSE'S CHRISTMAS GIFT
by Tina Beckett
THE MIDWIFE'S PREGNANCY MIRACLE
by Kate Hardy
WHITE CHRISTMAS FOR THE SINGLE MUM
by Susanne Hampton

All available now!

MILLS & BOON®
Large Print Medical

July

Falling for Her Wounded Hero	Marion Lennox
The Surgeon's Baby Surprise	Charlotte Hawkes
Santiago's Convenient Fiancée	Annie O'Neil
Alejandro's Sexy Secret	Amy Ruttan
The Doctor's Diamond Proposal	Annie Claydon
Weekend with the Best Man	Leah Martyn

August

Their Meant-to-Be Baby	Caroline Anderson
A Mummy for His Baby	Molly Evans
Rafael's One Night Bombshell	Tina Beckett
Dante's Shock Proposal	Amalie Berlin
A Forever Family for the Army Doc	Meredith Webber
The Nurse and the Single Dad	Dianne Drake

September

Their Secret Royal Baby	Carol Marinelli
Her Hot Highland Doc	Annie O'Neil
His Pregnant Royal Bride	Amy Ruttan
Baby Surprise for the Doctor Prince	Robin Gianna
Resisting Her Army Doc Rival	Sue MacKay
A Month to Marry the Midwife	Fiona McArthur